TREASURES

TREASURES

Book 1 of
The Frencolian Chronicles

Carolyn Ann Aish

Horizon House Publishers
Camp Hill, Pennsylvania

Horizon House Publishers
3825 Hartzdale Drive
Camp Hill, PA 17011

ISBN: 0-88965-089-6
LOC Catalog Card Number: 90-86249
© 1991 by Horizon House Publishers
All Rights Reserved
Printed in the United States of America

91 92 93 94 95   5 4 3 2 1

Cover illustration © by Karl Foster

Scripture taken from
THE AUTHORIZED KING JAMES VERSION.

Dedicated to:

The 1989 Blessings Club Children

Edward, Amber-Jayne, Daniel, Diane, Jackie, Joel, Karl, Krystal, Kyla, Logan, Mark, who were the motivation for me to write the novel Treasures.

Special thanks to my daughter, Deborah, for her assistance in polishing the manuscript.

Jobyna

The feminine for Job; afflicted, persecuted.
As the gem cannot be polished without
friction, so man cannot be perfected
without trials.

Luke

Light; bearer of light or knowledge.
Spiritual truth can convert the darkness
of ignorance into light and intelligence.

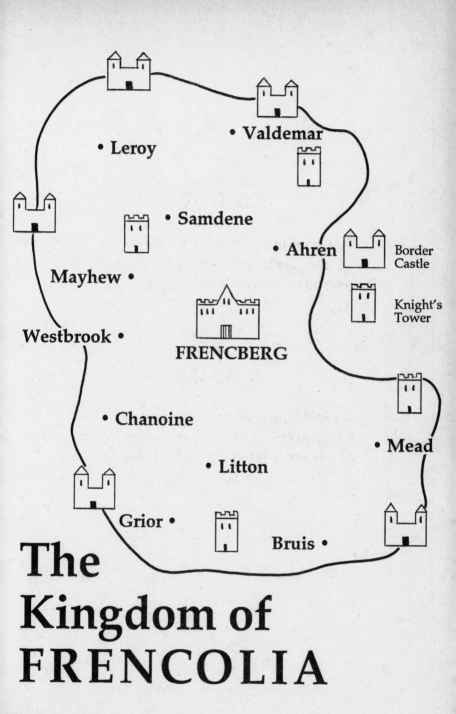

• Leroy

• Valdemar

• Samdene

• Ahren

Border
Castle

Knight's
Tower

Mayhew •

Westbrook •

FRENCBERG

• Chanoine

• Mead

• Litton

Grior •

Bruis •

The Kingdom of FRENCOLIA

1

Luke and Jobyna looked around the cave in astonishment. Luke used the flint kit in his pouch and lit two of the wall lamps. Jobyna heaved a sigh of relief as the yellow light crept its way to the dark corners of the cavern. The sight of what was in the cave caused their eyes to grow wider and wider with amazement.

Taking one of the wall lamps out of its holder, Luke started toward the back of the cave where in the farthest corner he saw chests, one upon the other. Passing the lamp to Jobyna, he cast his eyes on the largest chest. He let his hands wander over the top. The latches were ice-cold to his touch. Jobyna's breath thundered in his ears as he gingerly attempted to lift the lid. To Luke's relief, it opened with little more than a mouse-size-squeak.

"It's the same as the other one, Jo, full of coins, jewels, treasures . . . " His words were lost as Jobyna gave a blood-curdling scream.

Luke spun around, his hand automatically pulling a dagger from the sheath at his waist. He assumed the stance of one ready to attack.

"There's someone . . . behind . . . that . . . chest—over there!" Jobyna stammered.

Luke turned his head. The great opening to the treasure cave was still shut. He narrowed his eyes to focus in the dimness. The boy could just make out a form—someone or something, sitting, leaning . . . not moving.

"Come out! Now!—If you're man enough!" Luke commanded into the darkness. Jobyna crouched behind the chests. The form did not move. Luke waited.

"Hand me the lamp, Jo," he whispered, motioning with his left hand, not taking his eyes off the "enemy." Jobyna inched forward and put the lamp into Luke's outstretched hand. His breath came faster as he swung the flame in front of him. The figure behind the chests did not stir. It seemed to be slumped over at a strange angle.

Luke hesitantly took a step closer. Still no movement from the "thing." Luke took another step forward. He could now make out the form a little clearer. It had the appearance of a man with his head resting on his arm. Luke thought, *Maybe he is sick.*

He called out, "Hey, you! Who are you?" There was no answer. Luke waited. His gut-feeling told him there was something strange about this whole thing.

Jobyna approached behind Luke, who took another unsteady step toward the inert shape. He was only a few feet away and could feel his heart pounding behind his ribs. With the lamp raised above his head, Luke could clearly see it was indeed a human frame, a man.

"Be careful Luke, maybe it is a trick!" Jobyna hissed. "Look at the clothes he is wearing!"

Luke took a deep breath. Mustering up all the courage he had, Luke leaped upon the chest and kicked the shoulder of the man.

"He's got to be dead!" Luke said excitedly as the body fell backward. In great relief, he sheathed the knife he had held at the ready.

Jobyna gasped as the "face" grimaced at them. The eyes were closed; the mouth gaped open, revealing a distended tongue surrounded by shrunken gums and missing teeth. A look of agony pervaded the dry, leathery face—the skin opaque across the cheek bones. The forehead was wrinkled in deepest worry.

"Why, he's been dead for months and months," Luke exclaimed as he held the flame close to the face. "He's dried out!" The skin had the look of parchment left out in the sun too

3

long—like it would disintegrate at the lightest touch.

Jobyna's legs grew weak as she sank slowly to the ground. All this was like an extra nightmare, adding to the many they had experienced over the last week.

Luke's attention was on the chest. This chest was different from the others. It had a flat top with several unusual items laid out on it: a scroll, a ring, a quill pen, an open bottle of dried ink, a large jeweled case and a beautiful gold medallion with an emblem raised in gold upon it. Embedded in the gold were precious stones: diamonds, rubies, sapphires and emeralds. The medallion truly was a thing of magnificent beauty.

Luke picked it up and examined it closely in the lamplight. He seemed mesmerized by the glimmer of the jewels in the lamplight. The medallion was unlatched, a small padlock and key attached to one end. With his mind still on the luster of the gems, Luke put it around his neck and snapped the padlock closed. He held the lamp close to himself, turning slowly back and forth, watching the adornment flash colors on the cave walls. "Little sister, now what do you think of this?" he said grinning at Jobyna. "Look at your big brother!"

Jobyna gazed at the splendor of the medallion. "I don't like it!" she replied in an annoyed tone of voice. "You shouldn't have put it on. It belongs to . . . to . . . that man! That dead man!"

4

She shuddered, adding, "It might even be cousin Leopold. . . . " Luke held his lamp close to the face again and said, "Not cousin Leopold . . . unless he lost his hair, and shrank a lot! It couldn't be Samuel, either; it's far too small . . . too skinny. . . . Look, he has no flesh, just bone under the skin . . . " The boy stared closer and said, "Maybe this man stole the king's clothes. . . . Look at the size of those gems!"

Jobyna shivered as she said, "Come away Luke! Please don't touch him!" The girl was thinking of their father's cousin, the king, who had disappeared almost two years ago. She murmured, "He would be smaller . . . it's nearly two years; he wouldn't be much more than skeleton. . . . I hope it isn't cousin Leopold . . . I wish he would come back."

Luke broke into her musing, "Look, Jo! Don't you see? We're rich! All this is ours!" Luke spoke as in a trance, his eyes sparking like the gems.

"Luke! You're not in reality. How can this belong to us? We could never use it, anyway!" Jobyna's voice sounded a long way away, as though she was speaking through a long tunnel.

Luke walked over to the opposite wall of the cave. "Well, first of all, I'm going to light these lamps," he said. Luke lit one and handed it to his sister. "Now we'll take a closer look at those coins in the chests," he said. "If it is the coinage of our country, the first thing I'll do is go and buy some more bread; ours is so stale. Gold will go a long way to buy our way out of our predicament. Think of what the Frencolian knights would do for a bag of coins!"

"Luke, you wouldn't think of bribery, would you?"

Luke did not answer, so Jobyna continued, "Luke, surely God didn't bring us here just to use all this for—bribery!" Jobyna spat the word as if it left a bad taste in her mouth. As far as she was concerned, the matter was closed. Yawning, she stretched and looked for a place where she could settle.

Luke remained silent. He was terribly hungry and desperately tired. As he lit the lamps around the walls, Luke wondered if this was all a horrible dream. Maybe someone was torturing him, and all that had happened lately was just a suggestion to his confused mind. His hand flew to his neck. His fingers crept down the row of gold pieces and clutched the medallion. He squeezed until it dug into his hand, making the reality of it shoot up his arm. No! All of this was—incredibly—real! Luke scooped a handful of the shiny gold pieces. Sure enough, the K/F on the face with the image of King Leopold meant these were going to be very, very useful to his sister and him.

"Little sister, we need to sleep, and then, when it is light, I will go to the village or a manor farm and us buy some food." He picked up the leather water bottle and they shared a drink.

"I don't want you to leave me here, Luke!" Jobyna said suddenly feeling wide awake. The events of the past week were whirling around in her head. She cried, "You will be killed . . . like Papa . . . and Mother." Jobyna sobbed loudly, then said, "If they . . . are . . . dead . . . then they will be . . . in heaven!"

In the middle of her lamenting, she began praying, "Oh, God! Don't let them be dead! Keep us safe from our enemies . . . if we are found, help us to be strong." She broke into uncontrollable weeping.

Luke moved to comfort her; putting his arm around her he said, "God will take care of us." The boy's voice was unsure and full of tremors.

"Why . . . didn't He . . . take care of . . . of . . . Papa . . . and Mother." Jobyna sobbed, her body racking with spasms as she struggled for a breath with each word. She leaned her head into Luke's chest.

Luke's parents had been murdered by King Elliad, a self-pronounced king, who had taken the kingdom over after King Leopold Friedrich had disappeared. Many volumes of God's Word—and many Christians' lives—had been destroyed by the evil dictator!

Jobyna and Luke were fugitives, hunted to be killed, for the purpose of ridding the country of the last descendants of the Friedrich Dynasty.

Suddenly, Luke thrust his sister roughly from

him, feeling the hot tears that coursed down his own cheeks. He sniffed and said gruffly, "He has . . . He is . . . God has them in His care." The boy moved away, totally overcome with grief himself. Turning toward the chest, he struggled to pull his mind from the dastardly murder of his parents.

The sound of a chest creaking open came to Jobyna's ears. Luke dug his hands deep into the jewels. As he tinkered with the gems, Luke thought, *If that body is cousin Leopold, then the knights need to know! Father never said, but I know there were rumors that Elliad may have murdered cousin Leopold so he could become king!*

Luke's mind switched suddenly and he said aloud, "I hope they don't find the Gospel Books! Father hid them in a secret panel, in the wall of his bed chamber! If those books are destroyed, then all is lost for Frencolia!"

Jobyna rubbed her eyes. She asked, "Why do you say 'all is lost'?"

Luke answered, "Theon the Evangelist gave those books to Father six years ago when he became a believer. Elliad has been collecting all the copies and originals. Sabin said he wants to remove the religious words completely from Frencolia! If that happens, and Elliad continues with his reign of murder and injustice . . . that is what I mean . . . all will be lost! If only cousin Leopold had believed and followed the book! If only Father. . . . "

Jobyna was sleepy now, and she said, "Papa said it is wrong to say . . . 'If'."

"Well, he said it himself many times!" Luke interrupted stubbornly. He leaned his back against the rough wood of the chest, thinking.

Jobyna's thoughts stayed within her mind as she settled down to sleep. *Tomorrow, we will read that scroll. Maybe it will tell us who the dead man is!*

Luke's mind drifted between wakefulness and sleep. *Here was the "secret" that Sabin thought was in the valley and which he had urged me to search for! A secret once known to my father! Some "secret"—a cave full of treasures! Jobyna was right, though—what use was all this?*

Frencolia's future would be dark indeed if the light of God's Word was removed! King Leopold had once said, "If the Gospel Book was truly put into practice in the lives of everyone in the kingdom of Frencolia, then all my troubles would be over." His greatest reservations had been centered on other kingdoms close by who had their jealous and murderous eyes upon his kingdom. How could a religion of love and peace work when there were butchering enemies around who would rather spill blood than waste time on conversation?

Luke's mind flew to Sabin, the faithful servant who had brought them to the safety of the secret valley. He had gone to buy food and had not returned! Regardless of Jobyna's plea, Luke knew he must leave the valley. If Sabin had

9

been captured, he may be tortured and thus reveal their hiding place! With a bag of gold from this chamber, Luke was sure he could bribe his way out of any situation! His final thoughts as he fell asleep, rose from his stomach! How hungry he was! Yes! Tomorrow he would ride out and make some necessary purchases!

2

Jobyna awoke to the sound of tinkling coins. Rubbing the sleep from her eyes, she spied Luke searching through the chests. Most of the lamps were lit and she could see beautiful clothes strewn all over the place. Jobyna rose from her "bed" and examined some of the outfits and cloaks Luke had piled on the stone floor. Most were studded with jewels, gold threads woven here and there in intricate designs.

"And I thought the chests were all full of gold," Luke exclaimed. "Over half have clothes in them. Look, Jo, here are some ladies' gowns." Jobyna was amazed at the gowns. She had never seen anything so exquisite before.

"Aren't they beautiful!" she said with awe in her voice. "Mother had some beautiful clothes, but nothing like this. Luke, these must have belonged to someone . . . and we need to find out who that dead man is." She looked around the cave, as though expecting the man to rise up and speak out. "But how will we know?"

"I'll tell you what to do, little sister," Luke said as he walked over to the chest by the dead man. "Here, you take this scroll and the case. They will give you something to do today. Let's go out into the fresh air. There's some bread left in the pack we put in the first cave. It's a bit stale, but it's better than nothing." He put a handful of coins in a money-bag he found among the clothing.

Picking up the water bottle, Luke walked towards the wall that they had come in through. "Now," he continued, "to find how to get out of here." The two knobs were now on their side of the wall. "I'll just blow out all the lamps, and, oh, I'd better leave this here." He put down the things he was carrying and tried to pull the medallion over his head. Turning the necklace around, he called, "Here, Jo, there's a key on this chain. Undo the lock for me, will you?"

Jobyna put the scroll and the jeweled case down on the floor by the wall and tried to fit the key into the tiny padlock.

"It won't go in, Luke," she said. "The key is too big."

"Well," Luke said quizzically, "then, I wonder why it's got a key on it at all?" Luke pushed the necklace under his heavy wool tunic. "I'll just have to wear it, won't I, until we find a way to get it off!"

Luke grasped the two knobs and they found themselves on the other side of the treasure cave. Luke looked cautiously out through the heavy greenery.

"There's no one out in the valley. The sun is just coming up over the clifftop," Luke said, turning to Jobyna. "I'm going to ride Speed to the nearest village and buy some food. I'll also see if I can find Sabin."

"Luke, please do be careful! I wish we didn't have to use that money; it belongs to someone else!" Jobyna was trying not to show how upset she was about Luke leaving her there alone. "What will I do if someone comes in here, Luke?" she asked fearfully. "People must know about this place . . . Sabin did."

"Just keep near the cave. You can see the entrance from there," Luke reassured her. "The scroll seems to have a lot of writing on it. See if you can find what it is all about. Go back into the treasure cave if someone comes. I'm sure very few people know about that cave! Just make sure you have both hands on the two knobs at once and the wall will turn around."

"But didn't Sabin say we should stay here for a few days, Luke? I don't know if it is very safe for you to go out!" Jobyna protested sulkily.

She wanted to tell him that he was all she had left in the world; she wanted him to know she would not be able to go on living if anything happened to him. Everything within her longed for him to know she was finding life difficult. She could not bear the thought of him facing danger again.

Luke acted as though he did not hear Jobyna talking. He whistled for his horse, Speed. With a wave of his hand he was soon gone, leading the horse through the narrow opening in the cliffs.

Jobyna was overwhelmed with a feeling of loneliness and fear. Death and suffering were not strangers to Luke and her. Just over three years ago, a terrible plague had swept their country. Luke and Jobyna had two older brothers and a sister. All three had died of the plague. The king's wife and his four children had also died of the plague as well as many servants and slaves. Luke and Father had helped the knights with the burying of the dead. More people in the kingdom had succumbed to the plague than those left to enshrine them! Maybe that was why Luke reacted so calmly to the dead man in the treasure cave. Most of the country thought King Leopold may have become sick with the plague and fallen somewhere to die.

The thought of the body in the cave brought Jobyna back to reality. She decided to explore the valley some more and spend time with her horse, Brownlea.

While Jobyna was stroking and caressing Brownlea, she remembered the jeweled case and the scroll. Luke wanted her to read the scroll. *I'd better start on it before Luke returns,* Jobyna thought. She climbed back up the rocks to the overhanging entrance of the cave. Bringing out the scroll and the jeweled case, the girl was fascinated with the way the jewels sparkled in the sunlight. There were two catches on the case and Jobyna undid these cautiously. The article inside, contained in velvet, delighted her immensely.

"A Gospel Book! How wonderful!" Jobyna said aloud, overjoyed. She tenderly opened the pages. Jobyna was so intent on the Bible, she did not notice the charts and maps folded in a pocket at the bottom of the case.

"What time I am afraid, I will trust in thee," she read, "O God, you have not forgotten me." Jobyna felt as though she had found an old friend. She turned page after page; the words came alive as never before.

The warmth of the spring sun, the peace of the valley, and the contentment God's Word brought to her heart all joined together and Jobyna felt at peace. With a sigh, she fell asleep.

When she awoke, she was chilled. The sinking sun had passed across the valley. She was now sitting in the shade of the rocks. Jobyna looked around. The birds were singing in the trees. The little stream was laughing lightly along. Brownlea was grazing selectively on the sweet young grass. Jobyna wished she could always live here. Reading again from the Gospel Book, Jobyna felt more at ease than she had for a long time. As she pulled her cloak over her skirt, her eyes fell upon the scroll which she idly picked up and unrolled.

"These are the final words and last testament of King Leopold Friedrich, Absolute Monarch of Frencolia. Dated the twelfth day of February, in the nineteenth year of my reign."

Jobyna was terrified. She swallowed hard. Her mouth felt parched and dry. She must think. Placing the scroll down, she climbed over the rocks, down to the stream. It was not considered healthy to drink water from a stream, but Luke and Jobyna had done so over the past week and apart from quenching their thirst, the water had not affected them in any other way at all. Scooping the water in her hands, she drank thirstily.

That man, in there, . . . oh, no! He must be the king. . . . He must be . . . have been . . . our cousin . . . . King Leopold! Jobyna felt horrified by the whole idea. Drying her hands on her skirt, she returned to the scroll and read on with a nauseous feeling in her stomach.

"I write this testament with my own hand and leave my ring, the King's maps and charts, the Gospel Book, the Seal to the Kingdom of Frencolia, to be taken up by one who is brave and strong enough to rule with wisdom and justice. The words of the Gospel Book are true and if I live, I will teach the kingdom to follow them. I have found out too late. I leave everything in this treasure room to be used for the good of Frencolia. One of the two men who know the way to this chamber must become king. The rights to the kingdom are in the seal. The one who wears the seal shall be the King of Frencolia."

Jobyna paused in her reading of the scroll. *Luke*, she thought, *Luke put . . . on . . . the seal.* She was constrained to read on.

"Be sure to work with the Frencolian knights to look after the affairs of Frencolia. May God appoint whom He will.

"Signed: Leopold Reinald Friedrich."

Further down on the parchment there was more writing, not as neat as earlier:

"I fear I shall die very soon now. Gilroy's wife, Morna, gave me a drink and then informed me of the added poison. She said I would die within two days. She was sorry. Samuel, my great friend and counselor drank of the same cup, but he is stronger than I, and has gone for help as I sit here meditating on my fate. I feel sure my 'friends' have been well paid by . . . " and the writing went to a scrawl.

Jobyna was sure the name "Elliad" was in the shaky ending.

Jobyna sat as one in a trance. *Luke!* she thought. *He is wearing the Seal to the Kingdom! I wonder what Elliad would think of this! We will have to hide until we find a way to get the seal off Luke's neck.* "Oh, Luke, hurry back," she said softly. "Dear God, please take care of Luke!"

She placed the Gospel Book back in the case, closed the latches and rolled up the scroll. Going into the cave, she placed the scroll and the case on the rock. Climbing up, she grasped the knobs—one in each hand. Nothing happened. Jobyna twisted on the knobs and pulled at them, all in vain. The great rock would not move! In frustration, she lay down where she had the day before, drew her cloak around her and drifted off to sleep.

3

Luke rode like the wind. He wanted to get as close as he could to his home. The earlier he was there, the less people would be around, although most folks were up at sunrise. He hoped, by chance, to meet Sabin along the way. As Speed climbed the last hill, Luke was eager to look down from a safe distance on his beloved home.

His mind went back with pride to the beautiful manor house and properties he should, some day, inherit. With pride, he remembered the way his father managed the affairs of the manor and the village. His father had ruled the small domain with wisdom and the area was a hive of profitable industry. Everyone was involved in the work, including his father. Good measure was always given from the stores in the village of Chanoine. People came from near and far to buy wool, cloth, boots and many other goods because they knew they would get a good product and a square deal.

Luke sighed. This was over. It was hard to accept Elliad had killed his gentle mother and god-fearing father. In Luke's thinking, it would have been better for them to have died of the plague than to be murdered in violence. There seemed to be no purpose in their deaths at all.

He dismounted Speed and tethered him by a tree near the top of the ridge. Leaning low, he climbed to the crest and peered across the slope toward his home. He ducked down quickly as he realized the area was a hive of activity. Soldiers were in all directions. A smashing noise came to his ears; people were swarming around the manor house. The smashing was the sound of men with axes, chopping at the house—his home! Others were carrying out rugs, bowls, familiar tapestries, clothes and furniture. It was all Luke could do to constrain himself from calling out, from rushing forward to stop all this senseless destruction.

He knew they were looking for the Gospel Books. They would burn them, and the house, if they were found. The manor house was well on the way to being torn down. Luke tried hard to quell the tears of anger welling up behind his eyes. He bowed his head so he did not have to view the devastation below. Clenching his fists, he pounded the rock beside him.

"One day, Elliad, I will get even with you. You have taken my father, my mother, and now my home. I swear you will pay for this!" Venting his emotions on Elliad helped to satisfy Luke's feelings of rage.

Luke realized the faster he left the scene, the safer he would be. He did not have a sword or a bow. All he had was the dagger most young men carried, chiefly for skinning rabbits and such. He patted the bag of gold coins attached to his belt.

Ah. Yes, he thought. *This gold will buy all I want, and more. Yes, and there is much more where this came from!*

Luke decided to go to Westbrook, a town several miles north. Taking this direction, he would avoid both his own village, and Litton, where Jobyna and he had taken shelter. As he rode Speed along the less-known paths, Luke made a mental list of the things he would purchase. He must be cautious and not flash money around lest he arouse the town folks' suspicions. People were wary of strangers. He would pretend he was on a mission for his master, buying provisions for a journey.

Yes, he thought, *that will satisfy the gossipmongers.*

Fortunately, Luke's nervousness did not show as he quickly and shrewdly made his purchases: a fine new bow with steel-tipped arrows; a second-hand sword, polished and sharpened so meticulously the edge shone with brilliance; a keg of fresh fruit juice; loaves of bread; cheese; dried meat and fish; dried fruit; and much more. Luke filled a newly purchased pack with all sorts of provisions. He was very tempted to buy some sheep for Jobyna, but thought better of it right at this highly pressured time. The town's people were good to him and accepted he was a trusted servant sent to buy provisions for a journey.

While buying the bread, the baker told him, "You should have gone to Chanoine. I hear there are bargains for everyone. The town is being purged of a mad trouble-maker and a whole manor house is up for grabs!"

Luke knew too well it was his own home the baker was talking about. He kept his eyes darting around the market place, looking for any familiar face, ready to run for Speed at the first sign of trouble.

Securing the pack to Speed, with a sigh of relief he mounted to return to the valley. He mulled over in his mind how he could possibly tell Jobyna about the destruction and plundering of their home.

He was brought back to reality by the delightful aroma of venison stew drifting to his nostrils. Tantalizing sensations reminded his stomach of the hollow feeling familiar to him. He guided Speed down a narrow street toward the inn. Luke soon found the stable at the back. Describing himself as the servant of a rich farmer again, he left Speed and the pack in the care of a stablehand, giving the boy a few farthings to keep him more than happy. He had placed some copper and silver coins in a separate belt pouch when he changed three gold coins at the town's money changer. Luke knew it would be foolish to offer any shop owner a gold coin because they would not have enough to exchange and suspicions would be aroused.

The only regret Luke had in his enjoyment of the hot meal was for Jobyna not being with him to share the feast. On completion of the meal, and hot broth to wash it down, Luke heard a commotion out in the street. Absent-mindedly, he joined others at the door to see what was going on. A piper was piping his morbid tones as some poor beggar was being dragged along. Soldiers and a knight followed the procession. Luke had seen many a parade such as this, but rarely were there soldiers or knights present. This man must have committed a terrible felony to be escorted so securely. Usually the town's officials took care of the disciplinary matters, such as the severed hand he had seen nailed to the door at the barber's shop. Such a sight was common in these times. Luke had guessed someone in the barber's shop, (also a family home), cheated in some way and his hand was chopped off and nailed to the door to warn others not to be law-breakers. It was usual to dip the stump in hot tar. If the offender did not die of the whole trauma, he usually died of the infection that set in afterwards.

The procession came nearer. Luke drew back into the shadow of the inn's front doorway. He started in shock when the victim's face entered his line of sight.

Sabin! It was Sabin! Where were they taking him? What were they going to do to him? Throwing caution to the breeze, Luke joined the throng behind the soldiers. As they reached the town square, a hand fell upon his shoulder.

"Luke Chanec, of Chanoine, I believe!" Luke found himself looking into the eyes of the traitor, Tod. He wriggled and pushed to free himself. People around were used to such happenings and all joined excitedly in the "hue and cry" to hold on to Luke.

"Here's the one we really want! Over here!" Tod screamed. "Hey you lot, over here! Look around for his sister; she must be here with him somewhere!"

Luke's sole thought was to get himself free so he could return to Jobyna. He swung his fists, his hand hurrying toward the dagger at his belt. With his mind racing, he found himself dashed to the ground by a soldier twice his size. The last words he heard were, "No, don't! King Elliad wants him alive!"

Luke felt as though he were in a cloudy thunderstorm. There were lightning flashes, engulfed in inky blackness. He heard a harsh voice saying, "Wake up, wake up, Luke, son of Chanec. Wake up, we want to question you . . . question you . . . question . . . you . . . "

Another voice was saying gently, "Master Luke, . . . please don't die . . . don't die . . . die . . . die . . . "

A few hours later, Luke regained consciousness. He found himself lying on the cold stone floor of a prison cell with Sabin anxiously bending over him.

"Shh. Don't make a noise. There is a guard right at the door. He is watching to see when you wake up," Sabin whispered as he laid his hand over Luke's mouth. Luke was struggling to focus his blurred eyes. His head was thumping and his face felt swollen. He groaned. Sabin's hand clamped tighter on his mouth. The guard looked through the barred opening. He clanked the key in the lock. "Pretend to be unconscious," Sabin whispered urgently.

The soldier roughly pushed Sabin out of the way and kicked Luke in the stomach. Luke could not help moaning, but he kept his eyes closed and tried to lie limp and still.

"Well, at least he's making a sound now." The guard turned to Sabin. "You tell me when he comes around, or it will be the worse for you!" he growled menacingly.

"If I may speak, sir," Sabin said in a humble tone. "I fear he may die. Could . . . "

"No you may not speak, you worm!" The soldier back-handed Sabin in the face and went out of the cell, locking the door behind him.

Luke heard footsteps getting further and further away as the soldier left his post at the door. He heard muffled voices. Struggling to open his throbbing eyes, he said to Sabin, "How . . . did we get here?"

Sabin replied in whispered undertones, speaking close to Luke's ear. "Master, it was not good for you to struggle and fight so. The soldiers have been out looking for you, and were not happy it took so long to find you. El-liad has been getting very impatient with those who have been searching." He paused for breath then continued. "No, don't try to speak yet. If that brute comes back, it would be better

26

for you to play as dead as you can. It sounds as though they are changing the guard out there, or something is happening." Sabin spoke a little louder, realizing no one was at the door. "You see, they have sent a dispatch to Elliad to tell him they have captured you and from what I understand, he is sure to be here in person some time tomorrow. He wants you to tell him where your parents hid the Gospel Books." Sabin sighed, "I am praying they will go easy on us, and it will be quick. Tell me, where is Miss Jobyna? Speak quietly, now."

Luke tried to think. His head was splitting and he was feeling sick. The meal was churning around in his stomach and a dry, horrid taste sat at the back of his throat. "I . . . I can't . . . think. I don't . . . remember," Luke said trying to sit up. "I'm going to be sick." With three staggered heaves, he vomited venison stew and broth all down the front of his tunic. As Luke was losing his meal, soldiers clomped down the corridor, unlocked the door and entered the cell. Guards were posted on either side of the entrance, swords drawn.

"So," one of the knights spoke, "you're awake." He indicated to the older knight beside him, "This is the boy I told you about, sir." Speaking to the prisoners, he barked, "Stand up you two."

Sabin tried to help Luke to his feet, but Luke was suffering the effects of a concussion and collapsed into a heap on the floor. Sabin tried to wake Luke, thinking he was doing a very good job of "playing dead."

"You'll have to excuse the boy," Sabin said as politely as he could, "but he has been unconscious for several hours, and as you can see, he is in no state to stand."

The senior knight motioned to the soldiers at the door. "Carry him out!" he commanded. "Careful! I want him alive!" Pointing to Sabin, he ordered, "Bring him, too."

The room they were taken to was brightly lit and Sabin squinted his eyes, having grown accustomed to the musty darkness of the jail. Luke was laid out on a bench. The senior knight, who was addressed as Sir Dorai, gestured for the soldiers to close the door and be on guard outside. This order was instantly obeyed. Sabin and Luke were alone in the room with the two knights. The servant could see Luke was truly unconscious and he hoped his master would not vomit again and choke.

Sir Dorai pushed Sabin toward Luke, saying, "Remove the tunic."

Sabin, expecting torture, or worse, struggled to roll the tunic up toward Luke's neck. It was difficult. Luke was limp, lying heavily upon it. The tunic was wet, soiled and slimy. Sabin found himself flung out of the way. When Sir Dorai pulled out a dagger, Sabin fell to his knees, expecting his life to be ended. The knight did not use the dagger on Sabin, but cut Luke's woolen tunic from the hem to the neck, turning it back to reveal a magnificent rainbow of colors—the sparkling seal! The two knights forgot Sabin as they stared at the glittering jeweled medallion.

"You spoke truly, Raoul. Are you sure no one else saw this?"

"I'm sure, sir. It was I who removed his belt and boots. As I searched for hidden weapons, I felt this at his neck. I knew I must fetch you as quickly as possible. I've told no one else."

The two men turned to Sabin. Sir Dorai spoke first. "Where did he get this?"

Sabin did not have a clue as to what they were talking about. When they were hauled to the jail, he had been flung in the prison cell first, and Luke had been thrown in some time later. Sir Dorai pulled Sabin up from his knees and pushed him toward Luke. Emeralds, sapphires and rubies cast out rays of red, blue and green. Huge diamonds sparkled like thousands of prisms all around the room. Sabin's mouth dropped open. Never in all his days had he seen such a magnificent treasure.

"Speak, man! Where did the boy get it?" Sir Dorai growled.

Sabin tried to regain his tongue. With eyes still on the seal, he shook his head, stuttering,

"Sirs, I swear I don't know. I've never seen it before!"

Sir Dorai grabbed Sabin by the hair of his head and turned the servant's petrified eyes to meet his own. "Man, you do not realize how important this is! Look at me and tell me you have never seen this before and I'll run you through with my sword!" Sabin did not answer. The knight shook him violently. "Speak up man; tell the truth!"

Sabin found his voice. "Sir, by the Gospel Book, the Word of God, on which I trust my life, I tell you the truth. I have never seen that . . . that . . . thing he is wearing, never in my life before!"

Sir Dorai met the eyes of the other knight who said, "He's telling the truth." He released Sabin who again fell to his knees.

There was silence as the men stood looking at Luke and the seal. Sabin, realizing they were not going to kill him right then and there, dared to break the silence by praying, "God, You know I am speaking the truth and I don't know what it is that Luke is wearing. God, oh please forgive these men and protect us from evil."

The knights were oblivious to Sabin's muttered prayer, their whole beings absorbed with the thought of the young lad who was wearing what they knew for sure to be the one and only Seal to the Kingdom of Frencolia!

4

Jobyna awoke the next morning before dawn, feeling cold and hungry. The valley was misty and damp. A deserted feeling clung to the heavy morning air. Jobyna let her eyes run up the desolate cliff-face and linger on the hovering clouds. She lifted her heart and mind in prayer for the brother who had not come back to her.

Luke held a special place in her heart. There had always been a closeness between them that was different than with the other siblings of the family. This endearing unity of their hearts was the same for any two people on earth who are genuinely true friends. Jobyna would give her life for Luke, and although she did not know it, he would do the same for her.

The stale bread was not made any more palatable by being soaked in the stream water, but at least it was edible. Jobyna was so hungry, she gobbled down the rest of it.

Sun rays pierced the clouds, reaching their fingers to disperse tardy pockets of mist hanging sleepily in the cliff's crevices. Birds in the valley echoed their waking songs. It was as though the world stretched sleepy arms to awake from the last dreams of the night.

Jobyna savored the freshness of the delicate air as she walked to Brownlea's grazing place. She talked to the horse in a tender voice, and told him how lonely she was without Luke. The horse nuzzled into Jobyna's neck as she cried and softly spoke to him in despairing tones.

Brownlea cantered the length of the valley, keeping on the firm river sand. The weight of the girl, sitting astride his back, made him feel secure and safe. Jobyna enjoyed riding and it helped her forget her fears for a while.

A lone lilac lily caught Jobyna's attention, a sign of the new spring season. Dismounting to enjoy the fragile flower, she was dismayed to find it had been half trampled by a horse's hoof. "It's just like life, Brownlea." Her voice was soft and serious. "You just get to the beautiful part and something tramples it, spoils it . . . and ends it." She pressed the crushed flower to her sunken cheek. "If only it could be beautiful and live forever."

She rode up and down the valley for half an hour. As she once again neared the narrow entrance, her curiosity got the better of her. Leaving Brownlea, Jobyna walked up the rocky path. Coming out behind the waterfall, she squatted behind a large boulder. She could see a cloud of dust in the distance. There were horses and soldiers, quite a large company. With a pounding heart, Jobyna crouched down so she would be completely hidden. She felt riveted to the rock. The minutes passing by seemed like hours. Her mouth was dry with fear. With the thought that these soldiers may have Luke, she cautiously peeped out around the rock. The company had passed by and was going along another path in a different direction.

Jobyna breathed out a sigh of relief. She dared to try and count the horses. There were 10 at the back, eight ridden by soldiers. By their unmistakable armor, she could tell two were knights. In the middle, there was one person, a man, wearing bright purple, his cloak flowing out over the back of the horse. *Elliad!* Luke had told her he had dark hair and a brown beard. Jobyna felt sure it was Elliad, though she had never seen him up close. A knight rode beside Elliad and 10 soldiers rode in front.

She was thankful they did not know about the valley. Sabin knew what he was doing when he brought them here. Thinking of Sabin brought Luke to Jobyna's mind. Hoping and praying Luke would not ride into that company, Jobyna returned to her hideaway under the roaring waterfall, through the rocky entrance and back down into the valley.

The enchanting beauty of her sanctuary again filled Jobyna with feelings of worship for God's beautiful creation. Bringing the jeweled case out into the sun again and reading from the Gospel Book brought much joy and peace to her grieving heart. The words soothed, revitalized and strengthened.

Looking up at the clifftops outlined by the clear blue sky, she was thankful she could read. So many of the people in Frencolia were illiterate. Very few children read. It was only wealthy parents, themselves understanding the benefits of education, who taught their children to read. Rarely was a girl educated. Boys of "higher class" parents were groomed to be soldiers at the age of 16 and if selected would go ahead to train for knighthood. It was mandatory for these boys to read, for in Frencolia, the knights were known as the "Guardians of the Kingdom." They kept communications among themselves with regular, secretive newsletters, notes and bulletins.

Jobyna idly turned to the back pages of the richly bound Gospel Book. In the back there was a section: "Christian names and meanings." Jobyna looked down the list. She found her mother's name.

"Elissa," she read. "Dedicated to God." She searched for other names. "Jobyna—the feminine for Job—Afflicted, persecuted, as the gem cannot be polished without friction, so man cannot be perfected without trials." Jobyna was fascinated with the list of names and their meanings. "Luke—Light; bearer of light or knowledge. Spiritual truth can convert the darkness of ignorance into light and intelligence."

Jobyna read on; she was amazed at the number of names, many used by people she knew. The diversity of meanings engrossed her attention. King Leopold had written assorted diary notes in the back. Although Jobyna felt like an intruder, she read excerpts here and there, interested to see Elliad's name and home mentioned. Records had been made of her own father's meetings with King Leopold.

As she turned to place the Gospel Book back in the case, the papers in the bottom caught her attention and her eyes widened as she opened the first. It was a large map of the kingdom of Frencolia which included the placement of the valley. The northern end of the valley where the cave was situated was connected by a path marked "tunnel." This went through the cliffs, under the moat, and into the King's Castle. Jobyna's knowledge of maps and plans was limited, so she found it hard to work out all the details, but presumed many of the markings in the maps were secret codes and relatively unknown. Among the papers were plans of the King's Castle itself, with secret entrances and exits from the dungeons to various rooms in the castle and to other places outside the castle moat. One of the plans was that of the great throne itself with the words: "The key on the seal will open the step at the base of the throne, where the scepter and crown are concealed. The key and the seal are proof that the wearer shall be king." A description of a secret panel on the dais step was given, including how to open the panel to reveal the keyhole.

The plan that interested Jobyna the most was that of the treasure cave. The diagram showed six spots at the entrance. Arrows from each spot were directed at the words "key points." Jobyna gazed on the valley with unseeing eyes. *How can one person press six places at once?* Jobyna pondered. The answer to the otherwise impossible was triggered by the memory of the events involving Luke and herself a few nights ago. She realized she must have been lying in the correct position on two of the key points at the same time Luke was standing on two of the other key points as he twisted the two knobs. It would take two people, coordinating their movements to open the treasure-cave entrance. Jobyna lay back thinking, her mind mulling over the staggering discoveries of the past few days. Her body soaked up the warmth the sun had to offer. She let her thoughts drift away.

The dozing girl woke with a start. Papers were fluttering down the incline; one map was almost in the stream. The thin parchment was easily caught up and tossed about by even the lightest breeze. Collecting the scattering rebels, she carefully folded them and placed them back into the case. With the Gospel Book on top, she snapped the latches shut.

The day was dragging painfully. Drinking water did not satisfy the hunger gnawing away at her. If only there was something she could do to appease the deprivation her stomach was feeling. It was not the time of year for berries or fruit and the valley was barren of anything edible.

Brownlea enjoyed the second ride of the day and stamped with disappointment when Jobyna left him to see what was happening on the other side of her small world. The day was wearing on and Luke had not yet returned. She hoped Luke was riding toward the waterfall and would be there when she came to greet him. Almost revealing her presence, Jobyna drew back instantly when she viewed a countryside alive with soldiers on horseback. Daring to peep out again, she saw the soldiers rendezvousing and conferring. It was hard for her to imagine they were looking for her or

Luke; unbelievable that Elliad would go to such extremes to remove any trace of the Gospel Books and murder those who protected and lived by God's Word.

Jobyna returned to the safe haven the valley provided. In deep thought, she walked with Brownlea to the northern end. Near the cave, she had a wonderful idea and vocalized her thoughts to her horse friend. "That's what I need—a plan! They've probably got Luke and are now looking for me. Maybe Luke is still alive. I will have to do something as soon as possible if I am to try and save his life. I cannot stay here forever without food, anyway."

Jobyna got out the jeweled case and maps. She studied the plans of the secret entrances in the King's Castle, and the tunnel to the cave. Memorizing the various ways of opening the secret panels, walls and doors, Jobyna spent the remainder of the daylight hours absorbing as much of the information in the maps and charts as she could. Feeling sure the knowledge she had stored would be of great value to the right people, she drank of the cool stream water and settled herself for the night.

Long before dawn, Jobyna arose and rechecked in her mind the plan for the day. As the golden eyes of dawn opened across the soft grey sky, she brought out the jeweled case and the scroll. Rolling the thin parchment of the scroll tightly, she pushed it up her sleeve.

Some distance from the cave, she searched

the cliff-face for a suitable spot to hide the case containing the Gospel Book, maps and charts. Climbing a little distance up the cliff, she found the perfect hiding place. Placing the jeweled case inside a rocky cleft, she carefully covered it with stones and rocks. This took a long time for the young girl, who, although considered to be of adult ability, was still little distance from childhood. In a day when few people lived to be 50 years old, girls of Jobyna's age were mature beyond their years.

Jobyna took one last look at the wonder of the valley before she mounted the eager horse and directed him to the exit.

5

Luke drifted in and out of consciousness. His whole body felt black and blue, as though he had taken a terrible fall from Speed. He would just gather the corners of his evasive thoughts together to try and organize them and he would drift back into an unconscious state.

The next time Luke came to, he and Sabin were in the back of some sort of cart which was being pulled along by two horses. It was deeply dark; Luke could tell there were horses traveling behind and in front. He wondered where they were being taken. The night seemed to draw out into a never-ending nightmare; with each bump they passed over, pain ravaged his whole frame. Luke felt so miserable, unable to think of anything but the intense agony his bruised body was enduring.

Maybe, his muddled mind told him, *God has forgotten about me!"* With depressing darts attacking his mind, the journey of some nine miles seemed an infinite distance.

As they traveled, Sabin tried to calm Luke, reassuring him that everything was going to be all right. The servant noticed the incredible change in the attitude of the knights toward Luke since they discovered the seal. Sabin wondered what power it held over them? It seemed they wanted to protect Luke now, to take him somewhere safe. Sabin knew they were heading north. He guessed the journey must be important for the knights to be traveling after sundown. Very few people ventured on the treacherous paths at night unless it was a matter of life or death.

The soldiers urged the horses on as fast as was safe to travel. Sir Dorai rode alongside the cart, so he could check on how Luke was faring. The whole procession paused once or twice when Luke vomited violently. The beating he suffered was treating his body badly.

Luke imagined himself to be dying; he was sure he would be better off dead.

The clatter of the horses' hooves indicated they were on pavement and very soon the horses were drawn to a halt. Still semiconscious, Luke was lifted out of the cart by two soldiers. Sabin noted the difference between the way they treated Luke now and the carelessness shown when he had been dragged off to the jail by his feet.

Sabin's eyes investigated the new surroundings. Sir Dorai ordered him to go with the soldiers who were taking Luke. He observed that there were no drawn swords and no noticeable heavy security, as before. Looking at the large towered building before them, Sabin recognized it as one of the "Knight's Towers," a high tower-like castle set on a hill, used by the Frencolian knights as a center to guard the kingdom.

Sabin followed as Luke was carried through the open gates, across the courtyard and into the great hall of the building. The servant had heard of these Knight's Towers. When he had been a young boy, his greatest wish was to grow up and become one of the renowned Frencolian knights. He was from a poor family and there was no chance of his dreams coming true. One must be able to read to be a knight. To be the close servant and helper to one such as Chanec of Chanoine was a great privilege. Related to King Leopold, Chanec had been above the knights. Sabin accepted the way his life turned out, being faithful and true in his service. Back when the evangelist had visited his master, Sabin too, believed the Gospel Book message and his comradeship with his master was cemented forever. Chanec had trusted Sabin with everything, and the servant had vowed he would protect Chanec's family and possessions with his own life.

After Sabin had left the children in the valley, he headed for Westbrook and was captured there. Tod had recognized him and sounded the alarm. Sabin was being taken to the stocks to be publicly flogged and left until he told the soldiers where Luke and Jobyna were. That was when Luke's appearance changed everything.

Tomorrow, Elliad will come to the jail at Westbrook for Luke, and he won't be there. He'll be very angry, Sabin thought.

Sabin followed the soldiers up a great stairway and into a small room. A strange odor came from inside this room. Sabin had never seen such a chamber before. There were shelves all around holding jars and containers of every description and color. A tall bench was in the middle of the room and Luke was laid on it. Sabin kept his silence, knowing it was not his place to ask questions. He guessed this was where the injured soldiers were brought to be attended to. All sorts of stories were told in the kingdom of the cures which could be wrought in such a room as this. Sabin had heard about great gaping wounds being sewn up and broken bones being set.

"Listen up, I'm talking to you." Sabin came back to reality. A monk was looking at him impatiently, "I said, hold the lad's head still." Sabin complied immediately. Luke was groan-

ing and thrashing around. The monk wiped the congealing blood off Luke's face and neck with a sickly smelling liquid from a large wooden bowl. The monk rubbed ointment on Luke's bruises and wounds. To Sabin's surprise, he asked Sir Dorai to hold a lamp close while he looked into Luke's eyes. The monk put his ear on Luke's chest listening for some time. Listening for what Sabin did not know!

Sabin was surprised when he was given a straw mattress bed to sleep on, and he was even more amazed that he was allowed to be in the same room as Luke. Nevertheless sleep was far from the faithful servant. Although he was extremely tired, his mind was too active for sleep. The mystery of why they were brought here haunted him and left him void of answers.

Morning was a long time coming and when it did, Sabin paced back and forth. The monk had stayed beside Luke's bed all night, talking to the boy about all sorts of things. He had asked Sabin to keep talking to him and now and again Luke gave some faint sort of response. The monk seemed satisfied with any small flicker of consciousness.

Sabin looked out of the tower's arched window opening. The spring air was cold this morning. From this height he could see for miles around. He'd heard several parties of horses come and go in the night and imagined messages were being relayed, knights informed of goings on, whatever they were. Sabin had never been so frustrated about not knowing what was happening. He was desperate to have some kind of information. The responsibility of the two orphaned children was a personal burden he felt compelled to bear.

The tower window Sabin looked out was facing the east and he watched as the sun rose between the distant mountains. The town of Samdene was to the northeast, and he knew the King's Castle was south of that. The shape of the small opening did not allow much of a view. Although he could hear the clattering hooves of horses, he could not see them.

"Jobyna, Jobyna, I must go to her." Luke was trying to get up. He sat on the edge of the bed with his head in his hands. The monk pushed him back, telling him to lie down again. Luke lurched forward and tried to stand up. "I must take her some food, she has nothing to eat!" Sabin rushed forward as Luke fell. They forced him to lie down again, and while Sabin sat beside Luke, the monk prepared a drink for him. With Sabin's help, they coaxed Luke to drink it. The boy was soon fast asleep. To Sabin's relief, he was resting more peacefully.

With a terrific clang, the door swung open. Sir Dorai entered, accompanied by two men dressed in the uniform of the knights. Sabin was surprised to see Sir Dorai wearing ordinary clothing. It was hard to think of a knight being "normal!" Sabin had been given a plain tunic with an open front placket to put on Luke. When commanded by Sir Dorai, Sabin pulled the seal from inside the tunic so it was in full view. The men poured over the seal, whispering in undertones Sabin could not make out.

Sir Dorai turned to the monk. "So how is the lad doing now?" he questioned.

"Much better," was the answer. "But it will be several days or more before he will be fit to tell you anything you can understand. It may be even longer before he can remember much about himself at all. Someone really stomped on his head." The monk rubbed his hands together showing he was very upset.

"Yes, we know," Sir Dorai said grimly. "But we took care of that before we left Westbrook; we're a few soldiers less! Let me know when he is able to talk to us." Turning to Sabin, he beckoned for him to follow them.

Sabin followed the men to a room resembling an office. Sir Dorai sat behind a large desk. The other two knights sat, one on each side of Sabin.

"Be at ease, man." Sir Dorai assured Sabin. "We are not going to harm you, or Luke. We need to know all you can tell us about him and where he has been these past days."

The questions came thick and fast. Sabin was interrogated about his life with his master, Chanec, and his mistress, Elissa. They wanted to know about all the children, the manor house, the workings of the village of Chanoine. Particularly they asked about Luke. The intricate details of his life, his education, even his leisure time, his beliefs and values, his reactions under certain circumstances. The Gospel Book was discussed, and the way Luke's family sought to protect the book—being prepared to die for what they believed.

Food was served. Sabin, with some needed nourishment, began to stop trembling and unwind. The knights were relaxed with him and were treating him as someone important. To eat with knights! He would never have believed it to be real!

Discussion about Elliad made Sabin uncomfortable. He was cautious not to be too negative. With his sensitive insight, he realized the knights had reservations about speaking kindly of Elliad themselves. Sabin noticed they showed sorrow when he spoke of his master's and mistress's murders. He did not miss the way they looked at each other and shook their heads as though in frustration and discomfort. Sir Dorai, at one stage, left the room for a while, overcome with great emotion.

After the remains of the meal had been cleared away, a knight asked Sabin the one question the servant had been dreading. "So then, where did you take Luke and Jobyna after you left Litton?"

Sabin was silent. There was a long time of quiet. The servant rubbed his hands on the side of his beard, nervously. To tell or not to tell? He wondered if this was all part of a well-schemed trick. Three pairs of eyes were staring at him, waiting for him to speak. He looked at each of the knights, trying to imagine what this was all about? By all counts, Luke and he should be dead by now. Then Sabin remembered his faith; God was in control. He mentally decided to tell all, whatever the consequences.

"Well," he began, "while at Litton, I sensed there was not a good feeling toward Luke and Jobyna. It was not anything that was said. It was a strained attitude I felt with our presence there. A feeling we were not as welcome as the children thought. Younger folks do not always sense these things. Luke and Jobyna were happy to be with their friends—the children of Baron Tolard—and they did not notice the tension." Sabin paused, noting the way the knights were leaning forward, hanging on his every word.

"Yes," said Sir Keith, "and where did you take them?"

Sabin was quiet again. Once more the men waited, showing no signs of impatience. *I must not keep them waiting,* he thought, so he began to explain. "I trust you will bear with me as I start at the beginning. Years ago, before my Master Chanec became a believer, he was very close to King Leopold. You see, they are first cousins and my master was one of three who were heirs to the kingdom." Sabin noted the men looking at each other with satisfied glances knowing they were hearing what they really wanted to know. The servant continued, "King Leopold favored Master Chanec over the other two joint-heirs, Samuel of Samdene and Leroy. I believe he shared many things with my master." Sabin paused for breath as the men again leaned forward. He sighed a huge sigh, finally resigned to telling these men all he knew.

"When my master became a Christian, the king chose Samuel in his place as his close confidant." Sabin hesitated for a moment, to steady his emotions as he spoke of the master he had cared for so very deeply.

"One of the places I went with King Leopold and my master, was a small hidden valley, not far from Chanoine, lying in a high ridge between the town and the King's Castle. I did not go right into the valley, but was left on watch by the entrance. It was such a high place, one could see all the main paths for some distance. I thought of this valley when the children needed somewhere safe to go."

Sir Dorai motioned for Sabin to stop a moment. He rose and took a file of maps from a shelf and asked Sabin to show them where he thought the valley lay. On the map, the valley was marked as a ridge of small mountains. Sabin described the waterfall cascading over the entrance. They asked him what was in the valley and where the men went? Sabin said he did not know as he never ventured from the entrance. When questioned about the length of time the men spent there, he replied, "Sometimes it was a whole morning, or at least several hours."

"Sometimes," Sabin told his attentive audience, "they would return with maps and charts and books that they did not take in there. Oh, yes, sometimes Baron Chanec and the king would go in, leaving me on watch at the entrance, and when he returned, my master would be alone. This puzzled me greatly as he used to leave the king's horse tethered in the glade." Sabin felt as though he were telling a riddle.

"When King Leopold turned up missing, why did Chanec not come to the knights about the valley?" Sir Dorai asked. Sabin shook his head, trying to remember what his master had told him.

"My master wanted nothing to do with the rights he had as joint-heir. He kept quoting a verse from the Gospel Book," Sabin tried to think accurately of the words.

"Yes . . . ?" The men eagerly waited.

Sabin's eyes went to the ceiling, trying to recall his master's statements. "My master would say, 'God appoints kings and princes. As for me, I will pray for King Leopold and God will take care of him.' He said these words often when he discussed happenings in the kingdom."

Satisfied Sabin had supplied all the information they required for the time being, they told him they would like him to show them the valley, probably on the morrow. Sabin assured the knights he would be willing to do this, as he felt they might find Jobyna there. The servant was accompanied back to Luke's room where the men again spoke to Luke's caretaker. Sabin learned that Luke could still be a few days recovering.

Later in the day, Sir Dorai sent a soldier to bring Sabin to his office. Sabin was told to sit down, this time he and Sir Dorai were alone in the large room. Looking Sabin directly in the eyes, Sir Dorai cleared his throat and said, "Sabin, servant of the late Chanec, I trust you. I can see why Chanec confided in you. I have decided to tell you some things that ears such as yours never hear. To repeat such things would mean one's tongue to be cut out." Sir Dorai paused, making sure the severe warning had time to make its impact.

"The Seal to the Kingdom of Frencolia is something you have never heard about. It is what Luke is wearing. We must learn how he came to have it in his possession. The last person to have worn the seal, you see, was King Leopold Friedrich."

Reluctantly, Sabin listened, wishing in many ways he did not have to hear of such things. He considered himself a humble servant, not one to delve into other men's private matters. The less he knew, the less he would have to worry about. Never suspecting the servant's thoughts, Sir Dorai continued.

"The Seal to the Kingdom of Frencolia is to be worn only by the Royal Monarch of Frencolia. The seal gives the wearer the rights to the King's Castle, the throne, the treasury, authority over the Frencolian knights and power to reign over the whole kingdom!" Sir Dorai gestured speechlessly with his hands. He swallowed, found his voice and continued. "When a soldier is knighted, he sees for the first time, the Seal to the Kingdom. Part of his oath is to swear allegiance to, and promise to protect, the wearer of the seal and to guard all the affairs of Frencolia." His voice tapered off and became soft. "The oath of the knights is taken to be deadly serious. All knights are sworn to kill, without questioning, anyone working against the Seal to the Kingdom." His voice was now a whisper. "And to think, a 15-year-old boy is wearing the seal! And the neck it is on is Luke Chanec!" Sir Dorai paced the roomy office, trying to control his emotions again. He showed great confidence in Sabin, the servant, by telling him all these tremendous secrets.

"You see, Sabin, even if the king had a son of his own to be heir, he could not wear the seal until he was 16 years old. Even then his reign would be with the direction of the five lords of the kingdom, together with the 14 senior knights. The throne of Frencolia has been protected for over 200 years from falling into the hands of the uninitiated."

There was a deep silence.

Sabin dared to speak, "If I may ask a question, sir . . . ?" Sabin waited for an answer. Sir Dorai nodded his approval. "Excuse me if the question is impertinent, sir, but how did one such as Elliad come to be king?"

This question was somewhat embarrassing to a senior knight! Looking strangely perplexed and defeated, Sir Dorai, a tall, athletic, muscular man, paced back and forth once more. Minutes later, frowning, he replied, "Elliad is a self-appointed king. Without direction from King Leopold, and without the seal, the knights were at a loss to know what to do. As senior knights we were afraid what the lack of leadership might bring. The knights and soldiers could have started fighting among themselves and the kingdom would have been divided. No provision had been made for such a case and the situation was unprecedented. Elliad filled the need for direction and authority. Without this, I fear, the kingdom would have fallen apart. For the sake of guarding the safety of Frencolia, we voted to support Elliad. It has been two long years and we have not agreed with all Elliad has done, but he has maintained power and control of the country." Almost forgetting Sabin's presence he added, "But Elliad has much to answer for. He has not always looked after the affairs of Frencolia!" As if reading the next question in Sabin's mind, Sir Dorai continued, "I have sent out a confidential message to the other 13 senior knights and as soon as possible we are to rendezvous to discuss the whole situation. My recommendation is that they visit here first to see the seal for themselves and discuss with other knights what action we will take."

The senior knight looked at Sabin. "I do not have plans that I feel confident with, yet." He shook his head and sighed. "Let us go and see how the lad fares. Tomorrow we will make that trip to the valley."

To Sabin's surprise, the knight put a friendly hand on his shoulder as they withdrew from the room.

6

In the distance, Jobyna could see a three-way fork in the road. It was still early, and so far she had met no one. Litton was her destination—if she was not apprehended along the way. Like her brother, she had a compelling desire to see her home again. Frencolians were home-oriented. The abodes were their joy and delight. Often drab on the outside, the women sought to make the inside bright and cheerful. Rich tapestries and glittering wall hangings had adorned the brightly painted walls of the Chanec manor house.

It did not take long for her to arrive on the hill, the spot they secretly called "Spy Castle," where Luke had looked down on the destruction of his home. Luke and Jobyna had brought their horses here many a time to watch the comings and goings around the countryside.

Dismay and desolation filled Jobyna as she gazed down on the smoldering ruins of the cherished home where she had spent her short life. So Elliad had his way! Jobyna did not know where the three Gospel Books were hidden. She supposed they must have been found and burned. Grief and heartbreak overcame her now and she gave way to the flooding torrent of tears and sobs that racked her weakened body. It was her parents she missed the most. How could she go on living without them? The shock of their untimely deaths had not really sunk in before now.

Allowing herself to lament until there were no more tears, it was some time before she could bring herself to mount Brownlea. Without a backward look, she rode off. Nothing more traumatic than this could happen to her. If Elliad took away her life, she thought, then she would be no worse off. She asked God to take care of Luke, believing that he could also be dead by now.

At another fork in the road, Jobyna met some travelers, and when they said they were going to Litton, she asked if she could ride with them. The young husband and his wife were going to visit relatives. He told Jobyna they had recently been married and he wanted to show his wife off to his cousins in Litton. The conversation was cheerful and relaxed. Jobyna told them she was going to visit Baron Tolard and his family. They displayed surprise in Jobyna riding alone as this was not socially acceptable. Jobyna decided she had nothing to lose, so she told them the story about her parents' murders.

Listening in silence until Jobyna had bared her heart, the young bride spoke. "My mother has a Gospel Book. When the soldiers came to the house and knocked on the door to ask her about it, she put it quickly in the bread dough and it went into the oven. It had a leather case on it, and as far as we know, the Gospel Book is still baked inside the bread. They ransacked the whole house, but did not think of looking in the oven at the bread!"

It cheered Jobyna immensely to think someone had outwitted Elliad for once. They all held their breath as a dozen soldiers riding in formation came around the distant corner. Jobyna looked for a knight, but there were none with them. Drawing their horses off the path, they watched the soldiers ride by. Hardly a glance was sent their way for which they were all thankful. Jobyna did not wish to lead her new friends into any trouble.

As they neared the manor house at Litton,

promises were made to pray for each other. They parted before riding into full view of the town. The gates to the moat-bridge at the entrance to the manor house property were closed. Jobyna worried something was amiss. She could clearly see four soldiers on guard at the gate.

Jobyna rode as near as she dared. The soldiers did not move. "Excuse me," she called. "I am Jobyna, Daughter of Chanec of Chanoine, and I have come to give myself up. I would like to visit my friends here first."

The soldiers looked at Jobyna with vague recognition. She did not realize how much thinner she was and how drawn her face looked. They opened the gates and allowed her to ride Brownlea over the moat. She led the horse to the stable where the stablehands stared at her in wonder. Pulling the heavy bell at the front door, she was greeted by the chief servant, Ruskin, who glared in stony, surprised silence.

"Ruskin, remember me? Jobyna Chanec." The girl continued with reproach in her voice, "Please announce to the master that I am here and I would like to see him."

Ruskin opened the door further, allowing Jobyna to enter the small hall. She gave him her cloak and pulled her riding gloves off. He explained, "The mistress is here on her own; Baron Tolard went away with King Elliad yesterday."

The "welcome" extended to Jobyna by her friends was sullen and cold. Something was definitely wrong.

"Nita, Tolson," Jobyna asked her friends as she was ushered to the day room, "what is wrong?"

Nita explained how Elliad had come looking for Luke and Jobyna. The king had demanded all copies of the Gospel Book, threatening their lives.

"He said he was going to kill Nita and me first while Mother and Father would be made to watch," Tolson told a horrified Jobyna. "When one of the knights bound my hands behind my back, Father could bear it no more," he said, his voice tapering off to a whimper.

Jobyna asked the question racing in her mind, "He gave Elliad the Gospel Books, didn't he?" The somber eyes of her friends gave away the horrible truth. "How many? How many did you give him?"

Nita took up the story, "All five. Father was really distressed to hear how . . . how . . . your . . . parents were killed . . . and he did not want that to happen to us. He told us King Elliad can take away the written Word, but he cannot take away the Word of God that is engraved on our hearts."

"But what will your children do, and my children do, and their children do if all Gospel Books are destroyed?" Jobyna was exhausted. She fell back against the cushions on the wooden bench and cried uncontrollably. Nita and Tolson tried to comfort her.

After a while, the elder girl composed herself. "I cannot think clearly. The last real meal I had was with you, over five days ago. We just had the bread we took with us from home."

She felt faint with the sick feeling in her heart. It all seemed too much. All they had been fighting for may be lost. In the great grief she felt over the surrender of the Gospel Books, Jobyna wondered how God could have His way when Elliad was getting what he wanted.

Nita brought Jobyna fresh bread, cheese and milk, and it seemed to her better than anything she had ever eaten. "Mother has shut herself in her room. The threats of the king made her faint. Father was commanded to go with King Elliad to help search for Luke and you . . . and . . . do you know where Luke is, Jobyna?" Nita asked.

Tolson, speaking his thoughts, took up the story, "We did not believe the reports that came to us about Luke killing eight soldiers."

Jobyna interrupted in shocked tones, "What do you mean? Luke didn't kill any soldiers!" Jobyna realized they had missed telling her the whole story. "Tell me what you know from when we left here with Sabin."

The children explained to Jobyna what they had heard through the excited whispers of the servants' and the soldiers' children. News came through of Luke's capture in Westbrook.

Elliad had headed off that way, taking their father with him, and the five Gospel Books.

"He did not burn them here?" Jobyna was immensely interested in this.

"No," Nita took over the tale, "one of the servants said that he is looking for a special Gospel Book! He is keeping the others at his castle. They say that when he is sure he has them all, he is going to make a big bonfire with them!"

"He must be mad!" Jobyna exclaimed. "There is nothing more senseless than to destroy the beautiful words of the book!" She remembered the book in the valley as Nita's voice cut into her thoughts.

"He told Father he has over 100 Gospel Books so far and he is sure there is four times that number to be collected." Nita said. "Do you think there is a special Gospel Book?"

Jobyna decided not to answer this question and changed the subject, asking the question that was foremost in her mind, "What else do you know about Luke?"

"Are you really sure you want to know?" Tolson asked. Jobyna nodded, frowning impatiently, so the boy continued. "When Elliad arrived at the jail, he found that Luke and Sabin escaped, having left all the soldiers dead in the prison. There was no one alive at the prison to say what had really happened. Elliad feared Luke had captured a knight, too, and was holding him for ransom."

"But that is ridiculous, Tolson." Jobyna laughed. "Can you imagine Luke and Sabin accomplishing all that?"

"No," the boy replied. "Especially not when the first report was that Luke had been knocked out by a soldier in the square at Westbrook and he was half dead in the prison cell!"

Jobyna felt numb. *Where is he now then? How did he escape? He couldn't have . . . he wouldn't have . . . murdered any soldiers or taken a knight captive. A knight! Luke or Sabin wouldn't have a chance. Neither of them know anything about weapons or fighting!*

"Here is the worst part," Tolson told Jobyna seriously, "Elliad has put a price on Luke's and Sabin's heads: 10 gold pieces for Sabin and 50 for Luke, dead or alive. When that is officially announced, every person in the kingdom will be after them!"

Jobyna paced across the room. "I need to make contact with a knight, and as soon as possible. I have some information that may help Luke." She saw her friends' interested gazes. They had never heard Jobyna speak with such authority. "Can you help me find where I can make contact with some Frencolian knights?"

Nita and Tolson looked at each other. There were hundreds of knights in Frencolia and one often saw them when one least expected. But to try and find a knight, that may be harder than they thought. They discussed the Knight's Towers and talked of the one on the mountain-top between Grior and Bruis. There were always knights at the Knight's Towers. All the knights took turns in the watch that was kept from the towers. When knights took off their uniform or armor, they wore ordinary clothes, so that one was not sure just who the knights really were. Most had families and lived normal lives.

"I remember, I remember!" Tolson jumped up so suddenly that Nita thought he had lost his senses. Then he calmed himself and went to the door checking to see if anyone was listening. He closed it again and beckoned for them to come closer.

"One day I was exploring in the cellar and I found a room I had never seen before." He took a deep breath.

"Yes, yes . . . " Nita urged him on.

"It was a big room, with knights' uniforms, battle armor, swords, spears, bows, arrows, and all sorts in it."

"How do you know it was knights' uniforms and armor?" Jobyna asked him.

Tolson scoffed, "As if I don't know the knight's clothing! The armor has the special K.F. mark of the kingdom on the breastplate, on the helmet and on the shield. The uniforms are green with gold inscriptions and embroidery. You can never mistake the hoods and helmets they wear. No ordinary soldier wears clothing like the knights. When I grow up, I will be a knight!" He was triumphant in his announcement. "I asked Father why the knights kept clothing here, and he told me it was to be our secret and I was to keep it so unless it was necessary to be told." Tolson continued, "Don't you see? Some of the men in our household are knights! I am sure of this because there are always knights coming and going."

"That's true," Nita added.

"Yes," Jobyna said, cheering up. "Father had two or three knights who were around the manor house. They always seemed to be there." She turned to Tolson, "But how do we know who they are?"

"Ruskin will know, or his wife, Sabra." Tolson stood up as though to go and ask.

Jobyna cautioned him. "I need a quill, ink and paper first. Then if you can find out who the knights are, even one, I must have some time with him." Nita found the paper and Tolson left to see Ruskin.

After Nita brought the quill and ink bottle, Jobyna asked if she would mind leaving her alone. Reluctantly, Nita left the room. Jobyna dipped the quill in the ink and as accurately as she could, drew from memory, the Seal to the Kingdom of Frencolia. She hoped one of the knights would know what it was as the scroll said it was proof that the one who wears it should be king. Jobyna had never heard of the Seal to the Kingdom of Frencolia, and she was sure Luke knew nothing about it. It was obvious to her that the seal must be of supreme importance, but she was not sure to whom it was important.

Blowing the ink until it was dry, Jobyna carefully folded the small piece of paper and tucked it in the palm of her hand, closing her fingers around it. She peered around the door, telling the waiting Nita she could reenter the room. Nita looked at her mystified, and when Jobyna did not offer any verbal explanation, the silence grew thick between them.

Tolson came rushing in, "Ruskin says not to bother him with nonsense! He also said that if you value your life, Jobyna, then you should flee, or hide!"

"What rubbish!" Jobyna laughed. "I didn't come here to hide, and I'm not going to flee. I came to give myself up, even if it means going to King Elliad himself!" The children looked at her in astonishment. They conveyed an attitude of dismay; they did not know *this* Jobyna! She smiled at their serious faces.

Slowly and with finality, she made a statement they would discuss and ponder for a long time. "God will take care of me. If I die, I'll live in heaven. If I live, then I will die one day, and then live in heaven. There is nothing to lose."

Speaking directly to Tolson, Jobyna said, "Take me to Ruskin and I will speak with him myself."

Together they searched the house, but Ruskin was not to be found anywhere. Giving up their investigation of the manor house as useless, they trudged across the courtyard and through the garden to a group of small houses by the river. Tolson knocked on one of the front doors, which was opened by a stout, blond woman.

"Sabra, do you know where Ruskin is?" Tolson asked. She disappeared without a reply. Tolson shrugged his shoulders and waited. A few moments later, Ruskin appeared at the door.

"Ruskin, may I speak with you privately?" Jobyna asked the towering servant. Ruskin beckoned for her to enter the small house. "Would you mind waiting there a moment, Tolson?" Jobyna asked. Tolson nodded consent.

Two small children sat on the kitchen floor, playing with clay bricks. Sabra gathered the smallest child in her arms, beckoning the older to follow. She entered the adjoining room, closing the door soundly.

With a wave of his hand, Ruskin motioned Jobyna to sit on the wooden bench. Jobyna ignored the gesture. Drawing herself to her full height, she looked into his eyes and said, "Ruskin, what I am going to show you may mean nothing to you. If that is so, then you should forget you ever saw it. If you do know what it is, then I need your help." Jobyna unfolded the paper so Ruskin could see her drawing of the seal.

Ruskin's reaction was violent and left her breathless. "Where did you get that?" he screamed at her. He tore the drawing from her fingers and crumpled it in his large hand.

"So, you must be a Frencolian knight!" Jobyna voiced quietly, with triumph. Ruskin clamped his hand over her mouth.

"Quiet," he ordered. "That is not for you to talk about here. We must go somewhere else." He released his hold on her and regained his composure. He tried to mask the confusion in his mind. Throwing the piece of paper into the fireplace, he watched the flames destroy Jobyna's art. "Tell Tolson to show you to his father's office and I will meet you there almost immediately."

Ruskin spoke with an authority Jobyna had not heard from him before. He pulled his cloak about his shoulders. Opening the door, he put his boots. on and strode quickly across the courtyard to the gate.

Jobyna waited in the office with great tension on her face. Ruskin entered the office accompanied by two other men. One was a soldier and the other wore old peasant-style clothes. The soldier looked to be in his early 20s. The peasant was much older. His scalp showed shiny and red through thinning hair. He was tremendously overweight, with puffy cheeks hanging in folds and large pockets of fat pouched under his frog-like eyes. Jobyna wanted to question these men, to see if they truly were Frencolian knights, but she did not dare. A woman was not considered worth consulting in matters of the kingdom; it was a case of being seen and not heard. Ruskin was agitated by the whole affair. He paced to and fro. Jobyna did not know about the "dual identity" some of the knights maintained. To her, they were rich and powerful and lived that way. She wondered how a soldier could also be a knight?

Ruskin commanded Jobyna to sit at the desk. He pushed the ink and quill toward her and asked her to draw the picture she had shown him in his house. The other two men shuffled their feet impatiently as Jobyna took up the pen. The soldier-knight's eyes grew larger and larger, full of incredulity at each mark Jobyna made from her memory. They all spoke at once, in fierce questioning tones, demanding she tell them where she got such information. The obese man stood back, rubbing his double chin, observing the others' reactions.

When they had calmed down, Jobyna said quietly, "So, then, you are all knights of Frencolia?" The air was heated with angry debate. How dare a girl ask such questions? What right did she have to know of the affairs of Frencolia? Ruskin went to the corner of the room, talking in undertones with the soldier-knight. The fat man asked Jobyna where she had obtained the knowledge of the seal. Drawing out the scroll from her sleeve, she laid it in front of him.

"I know where King Leopold lies. This is the testament I found by his body." This announcement brought silence to the room. The three poured over the scroll; they handed it gently one to the other.

Ruskin asked the question all felt compelled to verbalize, "So, Jobyna, where is the seal?"

Deathly quietness pervaded the room as Jobyna informed them she would tell only those of Frencolia, in highest authority, the domicile of the seal.

Ignoring her presence, the men began to make plans to inform the senior knights. It was as though she did not exist. All three wrote furiously on sheaves of paper, sealing each document with hot wax pressed by their rings. The knight in peasant's clothes took King Leopold's scroll and tucked it into his tunic. He was just going to do the same with Jobyna's drawing, but Ruskin snatched it away, burning it with the flame from the candle used to melt the wax. The two men's eyes met and Jobyna caught a glimmer of fierce hatred between them. Saluting Ruskin and the soldier-knight, the portly knight turned and left the room. He carried several of the messages with him.

"I fear Julian will warn King Elliad!" Ruskin said turning to the other knight. "We must move quickly. Jobyna, get your horse and meet us out front as soon as possible."

"Where are we going?" Jobyna asked with a tremor in her voice.

"Do not be afraid. We will take you to the Knight's Tower near Grior. You will be safe there." Ruskin's voice was softer.

Jobyna said a tearful goodbye to her frightened friends. Mounted sideways on Brownlea, she waited for some time before the two knights rode from the stables. They were in knight's armor with the helmets closed. Jobyna felt sure of Ruskin and the soldier; somehow she felt secure. They rode out across the moat bridge and rounded the bend toward the familiar road leading out of Litton.

A company of 12 soldiers met them, led by an armored knight. The soldiers blocked the way. It was a tense moment. The knight drew his horse alongside Ruskin's. Jobyna recognized his voice and his size.

"We will take over from here," Julian said. He turned to Jobyna, "By the power invested in me by King Elliad of Frencolia, I arrest you, Jobyna, Daughter of Chanec of Chanoine, for treason against the throne of Frencolia." In an instant the two knights beside Jobyna drew their swords, accompanied by the sound of 13 more.

"Stop! Put your swords away!" Jobyna cried out in commanding tones. "I will go with you, willingly! There must be no bloodshed here. Take me to King Elliad!"

One by one, the knights sheathed their swords. Ruskin shouted threateningly, "You harm one hair on this girl's head and you'll all be dead!" Together the two knights turned their horses, retreating the way they had come.

Jobyna was left with the confrontation. Julian leaned over, his paunch brushing her skirt. He snatched Brownlea's reigns from the girl's gentle grasp. With six soldiers in front and six behind, they set off along the road toward Frencberg, the capital city of Frencolia.

7

Jobyna lifted her eyes to behold the cascading waterfall. The secret of the valley made her feel happy. As they passed by the rocky, pathless spot she had turned off to go to the valley just four days ago, she hummed a little tune.

Julian barked at her, "Singing won't help you none. Not when King Elliad gets his hands on you." He thought to himself, *Yes, and a fine bit of promotion I'll get for this easy bit of work. Best thing I've done all year is to become a knight. King Elliad knew what he was doing when he selected me to be in his special Watch Patrol at Litton. This is the second time I've been to see him personally and presented him with valuable information. I just wish I had that drawing the girl did. The king doesn't know what the seal looks like either. Won't that be something to tell him about? Still, he's got ways of making her talk. She'll be made to tell him where this seal thing is.* Julian rode along with a loathsome smirk on his blotchy bloated face.

Icy drizzle descended from the ominous black clouds overhead. Jobyna pulled the hood of her cloak over her long, copper-brown hair. The sprinkling turned to a torrential downpour and the cold drops trickled down her face. Before long her clothes were heavy with moisture from the late afternoon storm. Julian spurred them on, keeping the pace up, in spite of the splashing mud on the slushy path.

A mile or so ahead of this company another group was riding, back to the Knight's Tower at Mayhew. Sabin rode with Sir Dorai and three other knights after showing them the valley to see if they could find Luke's sister.

Sabin had never completely entered the valley before, but to him, it had been just an ordinary rocky place with several grassy pockets and trees by a stream. A quick search made it obvious Jobyna had left the valley. The girl's footprints were here and there in the sand, and recent signs of a horse were visible. One of the knights found a fine piece of parchment snagged in a bush. It was torn, the signs and symbols difficult to read. Sir Dorai placed it in his pouch for future study.

"To do a thorough search of this place, I'd need 50 men," Sir Dorai had said as he mounted his horse and beckoned them to leave the valley. He thought he might proceed with that idea, *or maybe a hundred men. Then they could turn over every stone in the place.*

Luke showed marked improvement today. He could take a little soup and although it hurt his jaw to chew, he managed to swallow some bread soaked in broth. Aided by two of the monks, Luke managed to walk to the door and back before collapsing upon his bed. They did not talk to him, except to answer his questions which were uncoordinated and repetitive.

"Where has Sabin gone?"

To which they said, "Not far, he'll be back shortly."

"Have they found my sister?"

"No, they have not found your sister, but they are looking for her."

Luke's thoughts were somewhat less jumbled today. He was making better progress than the monks expected. Most of the time he lay on his bed dozing. The monks kept a cold, damp cloth over his eyes. He was bewildered as to his whereabouts and why he was in such a place. When he voiced his queries, the monks replied, "You're somewhere safe. Stop worrying!"

Once, during a coherent moment, he opened the door and found his way barred by two soldiers. Luke retreated back into the room and asked the monks, "Am I a prisoner?"

To which they answered, "Not a prisoner in the real meaning of the word. Just think of yourself as a protected guest!"

Luke shuffled his way back to his resting place and laid the cloth over his throbbing eyes again. He wished he could remember what had happened. There was a strange blankness in his mind, an empty void he ached to fill. Every time he tried to think about his father, his mother, or Jobyna, it was as though they were pieces of a floating jig-saw puzzle that would not interlock, try as he might. His intellect could not comprehend the past at all. Something despicable had taken place, but his mind would not let him remember.

Aware of the heavy ornament around his neck, he sat up suddenly. The lad tried to pull it off, grinding his teeth with the effort. Restraining him firmly, the monks feared he might strangle himself. After administration of a dose of their medicine, he settled down once again in a restless sleep.

Upon Sabin and the knights' return, Sir Dorai entered Luke's room with the servant. Luke was suffering some delirium and did not know Sabin. The monks suggested Sir Dorai return later in the evening when Luke recovered from the effects of the draft recently ingested, informing the eager men of Luke's positive improvement.

Sir Dorai requested Sabin join him and the other knights for the evening meal, speaking as if the servant were an old friend. The meal was half consumed when a soldier briskly entered the dining room door. He saluted and announced, "A message from Litton, Sir."

Sir Dorai rose, almost over-turning the chair in his urgency to peruse the document. He hastily took the leather pouch, pulling a sealed roll from it. Silently reading, he sat back at the table. Without a word, he handed the note to one of the other three knights who in turn passed it to the next. Bypassing Sabin, the last knight to read the parchment whistled softly and handed the correspondence back to Sir Dorai.

"No reply just yet, but stay ready. Shut the door behind you," Sir Dorai ordered with a wave of his hand. Once the soldier had left the room, Sir Dorai read the note aloud, obviously for Sabin's benefit.

"Chanec's daughter to Knight's Tower, Grior. She knows about the S.K.F.—the seal—and where it is, and has knowledge of K.L.—the king. We have last Testament from K.L. Await. Signed R.J.B. Litton." (Ruskin.)

"Well," Dorai continued, "it's obvious the girl would know about the seal if she saw her brother put it on. They must keep her at the tower for now. We will ask them to send the testament here." Rising once again, he crossed the room to a small cabinet from which he extracted ink, quill and a roll of paper. Upon completion of his writing, he handed the page to the other knights who nodded their approval. After sealing the note, he placed it in the pouch and excused himself from the room.

"We must get to the girl as soon as we can. This mystery will come to an end if we can talk to her," Sir Dorai informed the wondering Sabin. The knights were treating Sabin as an equal, but due to his humble upbringing, his manner was distant toward them.

They had just completed the meal, when once again the soldier hurried into the room. "Sir, I did not get past the gate but met a knight from Litton who says that he must see you urgently. He's . . ."

Ruskin rushed into the chamber, his helmet in his hand. Breathless, he slouched on the nearest chair, taking great gulps of air to regain his wind. Not entirely composed, still panting, Ruskin described the events leading up to and including Jobyna's capture. He also explained that Julian now possessed King Leopold's testament. "I followed the company from a distance and when they reached the turnoff to Frencberg, I hurried here."

The whole matter was growing in complexity. Sir Dorai paced up and down the room. The last thing they wanted in Frencolia was a civil war!

Ruskin told the others about Julian, saying, "There are knights in Frencolia who, I fear, are not true Frencolian knights. I am led to believe Elliad has set up what he calls a 'Watch Patrol' of knights who are loyal to him first and last." He hung his head.

"What makes you say this?" One of the men rose and walked around to the back of Ruskin's chair.

"I myself was offered a large sum and a great promotion if I would join this group," Ruskin confessed.

Herewith great confusion erupted in the room. For the next hour or so the knights stomped up and down, verbally abusing Ruskin and cursing Elliad and Julian.

"How could we have missed this treason?"

"Why haven't other knights reported this corruption?"

"What kind of king is this man?"

"What is happening to the kingdom?"

"It makes mockery of our vows!"

Sabin excused himself from the ranting and ravings and climbed the spiral stairway to Luke's room. The lone monk now with Luke told Sabin the boy would sleep through the night. Luke had been experiencing some pain and the administration of more medicine had knocked him out completely.

Sabin imagined how Jobyna was faring and his heart ached with trepidation for the captured girl.

The ride through the capital city was a new experience for Jobyna. Intense sunshine broke through the clouds, causing vapor to rise from the wet horses and her clothes. Jobyna shook her hood back revealing wet hair, stringy with damp tendrils clinging to her sunken cheeks. Exhaustion combined with apprehension made her feel sick inside. Clinging to Brownlea's dripping mane, her tired back ached and her shoulders drooped painfully. She had never been to Frencberg before. Luke had made several excursions with their father, but women did not travel far from their homes, especially unmarried girls. The huge King's Castle dominated the area, and Jobyna was so absorbed with thoughts of where and what she was riding to, she did not notice the crowds gathering along the roadside.

"Death to all traitors!"

"Death to the traitor's sister."

"Kill the Chanecs."

"Down with all enemies of Frencolia."

People were shaking fists at her and the horses skittered uneasily as the crowds grew larger and louder.

"I knew I should have sent word ahead for reinforcements," Julian said under his breath. He ducked instinctively as a large stone he hoped was intended for Jobyna, almost hit him on his helmet. How these rabble knew it was Jobyna Chanec he was bringing was beyond him!

He yelled out to his soldiers, "Clear the way, clear the way." The soldiers, with the use of their whips, soon drove the clambering crowd back and subdued them enough so the company was able to continue more comfortably.

Jobyna's dread deepened as they rode over the moat and into the castle grounds. The whole place was a fortress. There were circular watch-houses all around the moat which seemed to go as far as the eye could see. Two more walls with two gates on each side of them stood between the moat and the castle itself. As they passed through the second gate over the moat bridge, Jobyna looked up at the great mass of towers and turrets. Nothing could have prepared her for this. Luke had said the castle was big, but this was beyond her thoughts of "big." The closer she came, the more terror Jobyna felt in her heart.

The last portcullis was lowered to the ground behind them. The thunderous sound it made as it hit the cobblestones reverberated through

Jobyna's mind. It was as though a door was shutting in her life, slamming out the past.

Jobyna found herself swung off her horse and pushed roughly across the courtyard. Soldiers fell in line on either side of her. Julian led the way, a triumphant look on his sardonic face.

They were met by two knights in uniform. Jobyna, though trembling involuntarily, noticed a different gold inscription embroidered on their tunics. The colors were exactly the same as other knights, but the initials were "K.E." Jobyna did not have to imagine for long whose emblem they were wearing.

"King Elliad has not yet returned from his mission," one of the men announced to Julian. "You will have to wait until he arrives."

Julian, indeed, intended to wait for King Elliad. He moved in behind the prisoner as the K.E. men lead the way. They went down a narrow stairway, unlocking a door on the next landing. The men stood silently on either side of the doorway. Jobyna hesitated. She was pushed from behind into the small stone-walled "holding room" for prisoners. The door swung closed behind her and the key was turned in the lock. Jobyna looked around. There were no windows, no furniture. Here she was, a prisoner in the King's Castle. The man who claimed the throne was not a true king and did not have the well-being of Frencolia at heart. As she sank onto the cold stone floor, the thought of her predicament pounded in her brain.

I am the only one in the kingdom who knows how to get into the treasure cave. Luke does not even know that, although he may be able to fluke it again with help from someone. I wonder where Luke is? Jobyna's thoughts were interrupted as her teeth began chattering. She was soaked to the skin, chilled and lonely. In her deep feeling of abandonment and depression, she was so self-pitying, she forgot the promises in the Gospel Book, and the comfort she could have in times of trouble.

8

Jobyna struggled helplessly. She was chained, wrists and ankles, to the stony floor. A heavy, ice-cold block of stone was pressing against her chest and she could scarcely breath. Everything drifted away into blackness.

A voice brought her back to the present, "Jobyna, Daughter of Chanec of Chanoine, where is your brother?"

She tried to see who was speaking but her eyes were blindfolded. There was a searing pain in her chest and the thought of torture came to her mind. *Is this what torture is like?* she thought.

Someone was trying to make her drink something. It was drugged, or maybe poisoned. She fought against it but hands were holding her down, forcing the liquid between her parched lips.

The next two days were filled with torture for Jobyna. She felt as though she had been trampled by a thousand horses. She could feel the pain from bruises all over her body.

Questions were thrown at her, one after the other. She was determined not to answer any of them. At one stage, someone removed the blindfold from her eyes and she caught a glimpse of the man who had been standing over her, interrogating, questioning. He wore a purple hood with holes cut for the eyes. His eyes were angry and glowed like rubies. Jobyna reached out her hand which was now free of the chains and tried to pull off the man's hood. Before she could retaliate, a sword flashed and severed her hand. She sat up, screaming, her body burning up. They were burning her. She had been thrown in a fire. The flames licked at her hair, her eyebrows and lashes; the perspiration coursed from her body. Again there was blackness.

Jobyna could see a beautiful garden with lovely lilac lilies, growing everywhere, just like the one she had found in the valley. A voice was entreating her. Through a delicate mist coming from the lily field, she saw her mother, beckoning her.

"Jobyna, Jobyna, come my daughter." Father was standing beside her, holding out a bunch of lilies for Jobyna to take. Jobyna hesitated. Where was Luke? She looked around. Luke must come. She must find Luke. The garden faded slowly into gray mist. She was lost and must find her way out of the haze. It was choking her! She couldn't breath! The sharp pain was there again. She could feel it, like a knife stabbing every time she gasped for air.

It was dark when Elliad arrived at King's Castle with Luke's horse in tow. He had sent out companies of his knights and soldiers to hunt for Luke. Two hundred soldiers searched every nook and cranny of Westbrook and the abandoned horse at the inn was connected to Luke from descriptions of the boy. It intrigued Elliad to find the supplies with the sword and bow that Luke had purchased. Residents of the town confirmed sightings of the boy and the shops he visited had been traced by the supplies in the pack on the horse. Elliad was traveling toward Mayhew to search further, when a messenger brought to his ears the news of Jobyna's capture. This cheered Elliad greatly and he returned to his self-appointed home with great eagerness.

"Well done! Good work!" Elliad was pleased with Julian. He had been briefed by the fat man as soon as he arrived at the castle and Julian gave him King Leopold's testament and told him of Jobyna's drawing of the seal. Satisfied his pirated catch was safe and secure, Elliad took his time enjoying a sumptuous meal, scheming how easy it would be to make this "Daughter of Chanec" talk. A little pressure would achieve much, especially from one so young. He was deliberately taking his time to add to Jobyna's mental misery, her solitary confinement without food or drink. It was late when he sent Julian and his K.E. men to bring Jobyna to him.

This was Julian's moment. The promotion and reward were already his. King Elliad had praised and honored him by requesting that he sit next to him at the meal tonight. He was gloating as he marched down the stairs to bring the prize catch to Elliad. Jobyna was to be presented to Elliad in the throne room before being escorted to the dungeons. How much more glamour there would be if this was Luke! But that would come, Julian thought, nothing seemed out of his reach. He was not prepared for the great disappointment he received upon reaching Jobyna's cell.

The men could not wake Jobyna. Due to the exposure and exhaustion she suffered, she was blue with cold. The physical and mental stress of the last week, the lack of good food, the tiring journey and the soaking she received that afternoon had finally taken its toll. She lay on the stone floor of the room like a rag doll. The men could not make out if she was breathing or not. Nothing they could say or do would bring the faintest spark of life to her frail form. Julian went empty handed, red-faced, to the throne room to inform Elliad of this setback.

Their little game was spoiled and Elliad felt greatly humiliated as he trudged to the room to see her for himself. He, the king, was going to her, the prisoner. What an anticlimax! The importance of the girl and what she knew came home to him as he entered the cell. In frustration and great anger he turned on Julian.

"Idiot! Imbecile! Haven't you a brain in your fat head? What made you leave her here in soaking wet clothes? Don't you know anything? If she dies, I'll have your head!"

Elliad barked out orders and Jobyna was carefully carried to a room where an open fire burned fiercely. He called in his doctors and threatened them with all sorts of maladies if they did not save her life.

Pacing the floor all night, Elliad could not believe what was happening, just when so much was in his grasp. How dare this disposable creature be sick like this! The doctors told Elliad there was not much hope. Jobyna's condition grew worse as each hour of the night ticked by and he became increasingly agitated. She may die, but he wanted to be the one to decide when; certainly not before he obtained what he wanted from her. It was ironic, he thought, to have to work to save her life before he could end it. He must have the information about the Seal to the Kingdom of Frencolia from her. He must find these "treasures" mentioned in the testament. He would do anything to make her well enough to talk!

Heated lambskin rugs were placed around Jobyna's still form and special medicines were prepared and administered to warm her from inside. A woman from the city was called in, one who was considered an expert midwife and specialized in children's ailments. Elliad offered her a great reward if she could save Jobyna's life. She massaged Jobyna's arms and legs with warm oil, working to restore normal circulation to the cramped limbs, shaking her head and muttering it was all a waste of time as the girl was scarcely alive and had no strength to pull through anyway.

The next few days were blustery and cold. The heavy rain was blown forcefully to the ground; rivers and streams grew to the bursting point. No one ever ventured out in weather like this. Doors and shutters were secured and home fires stimulated to burn brightly. Jobyna's condition remained critical, adding to Elliad's selfish depression.

At the Knight's Tower near Mayhew, news of Jobyna's sickness was received with sadness by Sir Dorai and Sabin, as the messenger said there was not much hope for her recovery. It was expected she may even die while the message was being conveyed.

Luke, however, was making wonderful progress. He was standing, holding the shutters open, trying to look out at the storm, when Sir Dorai and Ruskin entered the room. It was very early morning and still dark outside. The lamps were lit. The bruises on Luke's face were patterns of purple and yellow, a good sign of his healing. Luke had risen, wide awake at about three o'clock, unable to sleep. His mind was clear at last. The fog had lifted and the tunnel was behind him. He was still not sure where he was, but Sabin's presence in the room assured him all was well.

Sabin was fast asleep, snoring softly. Luke did not want to wake him. He had a lot of thinking to catch up on. He tried to piece together all that had transpired. At least he was safe here, but his concern went to his sister. He would ask Sabin about her the moment the servant awoke.

Luke remembered leaving the valley in haste. So much had happened since then. How unpredictable life was. He must never take it for granted again. What is today, may not be tomorrow.

He fingered the seal hanging around his

neck, remembering how impulsive and thoughtless he had been when he put it on. He wondered whose it was, and remembered the dead man in the cave. *Who could that man have been? How did he get there? What were all the treasures there for?* He did not know these questions would soon be answered.

A monk, on duty since midnight, entered the room as Luke was pondering these things. The door opened so silently that Luke was startled when he saw the man. Seeing Luke bright and alert, the monk left the room and went to Sir Dorai's quarters to tell him the boy was up and about.

Luke recognized Ruskin immediately. Sir Dorai was pleased to hear Luke holding an intelligent conversation. Sabin woke and Sir Dorai suggested they all go to his dining room and have breakfast. Luke favored this idea as he was extremely hungry. It surprised him how weak he was as he followed them along the corridor. His legs were wobbly and he felt sapped of all strength. His ribs and back ached as he walked. Sabin was joyful to see a change for the better in Luke and this happiness showed on his beaming face.

Luke could not supply the men with much information they did not already know. It was they who had news to tell him. With Sir Dorai's approval, Ruskin told Luke about the testament Jobyna had found and its content. Ruskin had carefully gone over every word, trying to reconstruct the testament, in writing, from his memory. He was angry with himself for allowing Julian to get away with this priceless document. Luke was amazed and afraid to know he was wearing King Leopold's seal. He was flooded with remorse for putting it around his neck when Sir Dorai explained the powers invested in the seal and the wearing of it. However, Sir Dorai tried to allay his fears, saying he felt it would all work out for the best in the end.

Luke said he wanted them to file the lock off the back of the chain. "I just want the seal to go to the right person so he can be king!" Luke said with certainty in his voice. Sir Dorai was silent, his brow furrowed in deep thought.

Believing Luke should know about Jobyna's capture, they told him of her sickness, trying to give him more hope than they knew existed. It was enough for him to sustain the thoughts of Jobyna being a prisoner in the King's Castle with Elliad, let alone to grieve that she was almost dead. Luke returned to his room, his mind bursting with the information shared at the breakfast table. He felt tired out. The fullness of his stomach made him sleepy. Sabin was concerned at Luke's drained expression, his ghastly pale skin, and urged him to rest.

The storm continued to rage outside. All out-door work came to an halt when such storms engulfed Frencolia. Travelers ceased their jour-neys and soldiers did as little as possible. The farms were deserted, the markets empty and people sat around their fireplaces resting, eating and telling stories. For those who could read and had access to books, it was a time employed studying and gaining more knowledge.

This was a perfect time for the senior knights to gather at the Knight's Tower near Mayhew. No one was out on the roads to see them come, and they could not imagine Elliad's spies being out in such adverse weather. The senior knights had not met since Elliad had crowned himself King of Frencolia. At that time, they voted, reluctantly, to accept Elliad and support him as long as he kept the interests of the kingdom at heart. Sir Dorai felt sick in the pit of his stomach as he realized over two years had passed since they last met, allowing Elliad much time to entertain his own interests and not those of Frencolia. The Gospel Books were one thing, but appointing his own secret knights and slaying innocent people for their harmless private beliefs was another. It had been tolerated for too long and the senior knights must take action!

All the next day men arrived at the Knight's Tower. The senior knights met in one con-ference room, and the others waited for the recommendations, then discussed them. Only knights sworn in for three or more years, were allowed to cross the drawbridge. Those not eligible were warned to return to their homes and keep the secret of the knights' meeting. The Mayhew Tower was fully stocked with food and provisions and plans were made in case of siege. Precautionary security was established against the tower being stormed. Although it was not stated, these actions were in fact against attack by Elliad and his men.

All was set for the most important meeting of a knight's lifetime. The outcome of the deliberations could produce a decision for civil war, Luke's life or death and Elliad being given the Seal to the Kingdom. Sir Dorai hoped the men would have Frencolia's interests at heart!

9

The storm reached its climax at the time Jobyna's fever finally began to break. She was soaked in perspiration and was hoarse from screaming in delirium at the nightmares she was having about suffering torture. The nurse, employing other women to help her, bathed Jobyna's fever-ridden body, administering a herbal drug to draw out the effects of the pneumonia. A hot poultice made with mustard, flax seeds, whole-meal flour, mineral salts and herbs was wrapped around Jobyna's chest and back. This was discarded and replaced with another as soon as it lost its heat.

Elliad paced up and down outside the sick room, angry at himself for not being able to think of anything other than the infirm wench. It was his one obsession to talk with this Jobyna. His control of the whole kingdom depended upon her. The doctor told him that to use pressure on the girl to gain information, at this stage, would result in her death. He must not let her die, yet.

While they were forcing the senseless Jobyna to swallow some thick syrup, King Elliad burst into the room. The women and doctors in the chamber curtsied or bowed low to him.

The nurse remained upright. Without taking her eyes off Jobyna, she said to King Elliad, "Excuse me, Your Majesty, but we will surely lose this poor creature if we are interrupted again. Every time the door is opened the cool air rushes in!"

Elliad moved to the door. His hands gestured impatiently as he muttered, "You heard her, shut the door and get on with it. Don't stare at me; get to work." He swung around and stormed out.

Looking at the situation realistically, he fully expected Jobyna to die and tried to get his mind back to some of the duties he usually performed when the weather forced him to stay at the castle. However, he found himself pacing the long distance between his offices and the room where Jobyna lay, fully expecting to hear the news of her death. At least then this matter would be decided one way or the other instead of being held in suspense like this! His impatient nature was at the end of its tether; he must pull himself together, he thought.

The news that Jobyna's fever had at last broken and she was coughing up phlegm was received with great satisfaction and relief. Elliad was oblivious to the extent of his involvement in his desire for her recovery. The great schemer and destroyer of human life was working to save a life for the first time.

Jobyna lay face down, her head downhill, unable to move for the pain. She cried pathetically as the large woman pounded her back with closed fists. Later she was sat upright, the nurse rubbing her back as she coughed up copious amounts of thick green phlegm and blood-spotted bile.

"Good girl, this is what we want." The nurse was pleased with herself. All her hard work and long hours had paid off. She pressed her fingers to her patient's lips as Jobyna tried to say something between the coughs. "Don't try to talk now; you must just rest and get well. You are a very sick girl. King Elliad has gone to a lot of trouble and expense to save your life. Just be a good girl and do what you are told."

The thought of Elliad made Jobyna's heart race as she began to remember where she was and why she was here. What would he want to save her life for, she asked herself? The nurse was spooning a hot sickly tasting syrup into her mouth. It tasted like fruit mixed with bitter herbs. Jobyna tried to tell her it was burning her throat, but there was no voice when she tried to speak. The words "do what you are told" echoed in her mind and she decided it would be best if she cooperated.

Filling her mind with memories of the valley, she drifted off into a dreamland of the sedated. The valley was the most beautiful place on earth to Jobyna so she allowed her mind to take her there and sit on the green grass beside the laughing stream. The drugs and herbs in the drink gave her a relaxed, painless, deep sleep bringing slow healing to her frail body.

Elliad stared down at the sleeping form. The nurse told him Jobyna would live. She would have to be nursed for several days before she could talk to him and the slightest upset may cause her to suffer a relapse. A relapse could be worse than the original sickness and she would likely die. The nurse informed Elliad that the girl's heartbeat was erratic and the fever might flare up at any instant. Elliad reminded himself he just needed to get the required information from her before she died. How was he to get her to tell him where the treasure was? His scheming mind told him to stay calm and to be patient. There were many roads to Frencberg and there must be other roads to achieve his goal.

The rains continued all week. At this time of the year it had been known to rain for a month. If this happened now, then the kingdom would just sleep on for a while and Jobyna could take as much time—within reason—as she needed to recover. He must gain the information from Jobyna without her relapsing. Elliad knew enough about these Christians to know they were not afraid to die. He would have to come at this situation from a different angle. His contriving mind began to invent his alternative strategy. A dog would not bite the hand which fed it, so this girl may confide in someone who was kind to her. Who would he choose? Who could he trust with such valuable information from the girl? How could he be sure this man, or woman, would not keep what he or she learned for him or herself?

The continuing spring rains gave an extended time for the meetings with the knights at the Knight's Tower near Mayhew. Luke was bored. News of Jobyna was sporadic and sketchy. His impulsiveness tempted him to try to escape from here and go to her side. At least they could die together.

The library at the Knight's Tower was stocked full of a great wealth of books. Luke found some consolation here as he loved to read and study. There were books dating back to the time of Christ. He read books about Rome, the Vikings and different countries of the world. Luke was surprised, and just a bit jealous, to know Sabin was included in the senior knight's meetings, but they treated him like a kid, and he was almost 16. Sabin did not even return to Luke at meal times and as the days dragged by, Luke found himself getting cross and resentful.

He discovered a Gospel Book on the library shelf. The cover was plain and unlabeled. He had not held a Gospel Book in his hands for so long. How the words cheered him. He read Psalms right through, all 50 chapters that were included in this Latin translation.

Sabin found Luke in the library. The lad had recovered from his negative feelings and spoke cheerfully. Sabin told Luke the senior knights wanted him to join them for dinner.

Luke was allocated the head of the table and Sir Dorai pulled the seal out from the boy's tunic so all could see its wonder. The servants brought the meal to the door. Sabin and some of the senior knights carried it from there to the table. Sabin served them all with roast chicken, pork, beef, potatoes and a large variety of cooked vegetables. Hot rice pudding was served with cooked dried fruit. Luke could not remember eating such a sumptuous meal for a long time and enjoyed the satisfaction it brought to his stomach. Sir Dorai noticed with pleasure the return of Luke's appetite and the clarity of the boy's speech.

With his goblet raised high, Sir Dorai pointed his arm toward Luke and said, "To Frencolia." This was echoed by the other men and Luke raised his goblet and pointing it toward them, said, "To Frencolia." They all laughed and drank to the well-being of their country.

Nothing could have prepared Luke for the meeting that afternoon. He had been blocking from his mind the thoughts and wonderings related to the men's discussions, knowing they would be including his future in their delibera- tions. They entered the conference room and Luke was presented to five of the oldest men he had ever seen.

"Lord Jamess, Lord Peters, Lord Farey, Lord Wolfer and Lord Shellac," Sir Dorai said as he made the introductions. "This is the boy, Luke Chanec." Luke shook hands with all of them, each wanting to look upon the seal. Lord Farey touched the jewels on the seal with trembling fingers, gripping Luke's hand for several minutes.

Lord Shellac kissed the seal tenderly and gripped Luke by the shoulders. With tears in his eyes, he said, "Praise God this seal has fal- len into good hands. May the Lord God bless you and be with you, Luke Chanec."

Luke was filled with wonderment; Sir Dorai said these men were the counselors of the senior knights and their advice was taken to be sacred. Sabin was not invited into this conference room and Luke was alone with the 19 men who, next to the king, were responsible for the affairs of the kingdom of Frencolia. The senior knights sat in a semicircle on an assortment of benches and stools. Luke was placed on a chair next to Sir Dorai and the five lords completed the circle.

Lord Peters stood to his feet to address the meeting.

Decisions had been made, votes taken and matters settled. Luke was not in this meeting to be asked but to be told. Sir Peters informed the boy in commanding tones that it was not up to Luke, whether he wanted to be or not, but rather according to the laws and decrees of Frencolia and the testament of King Leopold Friedrich, Luke Chanec was the legal King of Frencolia. They as lords and senior knights had agreed, for the sake of the future preservation of the kingdom, to fight if necessary, to have Luke ascend the throne. All of them had signed a mandate ready to be delivered to Elliad stating he, Elliad John Pruwitt, must surrender the throne, leave Frencolia and go into permanent exile. They would give him one week to do so and if he did not comply, war on him would be declared and he would be removed by the loyal knights of Frencolia.

"You are not 16 for four months, Luke, which is the legal age for you to be able to act as king in your own right and it is our suggestion that

101

Sir Dorai be your guardian and advisor until this time." Lord Peters turned to Sir Dorai and sat down. The senior knight stood to his feet, bowing toward the small audience.

Clearing his throat, Sir Dorai said, "Luke, there will be a lot of questions and maybe doubts floating around in your mind. For the time being, we want you to put these aside and trust us for the sake of Frencolia. There will be time later to answer your queries.

"Elliad John Pruwitt is second cousin to the late king as are you. Elliad is related through his mother and you by your father. Your father and his mother were not related; you have no blood tie to Elliad. By all written records, you have more blood rights to the throne of Frencolia than any other male presently alive and we take it as providence, or as you would put it Luke, God's hand, that you are wearing the Seal to the Kingdom of Frencolia. We believe that fate, or God if you please, has taken a hand to give you what is now rightfully yours and is at the same time providing Frencolia with the wise and just king you will grow into." This said, he knelt on one knee before Luke and said, "Luke, son of Louis Chanec of Chanoine, I pledge my loyalty to you as rightful heir to the throne of Frencolia. From now on your title shall be King Luke Chanec of Frencolia. In our eyes you are already king. The coronation will be a mere formality."

Luke wanted ask a hundred questions, but in

the gravity of the moment he lost his tongue. His mouth was dry and his heart beat faster than usual. The senior knights, one by one, pledged their allegiance and their very lives to serve him for the sake of Frencolia. Luke submitted silently to the dictates of the solemn ceremony. The lords did not kneel before Luke but came to him one at a time, each giving him their blessing, declaring in their own words their support of him as king. They entreated him to always "keep the affairs of Frencolia at heart."

There was silence in the room. All eyes were on Luke. He realized they were waiting for him to say something. He frowned, trying to formulate words adequate to describe his deep feelings. "Just two weeks ago, men of Frencolia murdered my father and mother at the decree of Elliad. My sister and I were being hunted to be put to death." Sir Dorai swallowed uncomfortably and apprehensively as the boy continued. "I did not think too much of the justice of Frencolia then. My father used to say often 'God will appoint whom He wants for king' and he would say that Elliad would be removed in God's time. If I am to be your king, then I want you all to know I hold to the teachings in the Gospel Book."

Luke paused for breath, wishing he had been given more time and warning to prepare for such an important speech.

"I pledge my loyalty to you, lords of Frencolia, and to the senior knights of the kingdom, asking you to remain my needed counselors and friends." Luke sat down, feeling exhausted.

Sir Dorai said, "Long live King Luke Chanec. May his God bless him with great wisdom and long life." All the men followed suit, saying, "Long live King Luke Chanec! Long live King Luke Chanec!"

10

In spite of the storms and gales, the Knight's Tower near Mayhew was the domicile for goings on such as never before. In fact, the bad weather served as a wonderful cover for the whole operation. Elliad was lulled into thinking the weather was his safety and it took some time before news of trouble came to his ears.

The lords returned to their various home towns, again taking great risks due to the weather. Many plans had been compiled, but the final choices were left in the hands of the senior knights. The soon-to-be-crowned king was included in the discussions, but Sir Dorai suggested he be silent unless questioned. He would discuss the details with Luke later, after the meetings. Luke learned these knights were men of action. In six days Elliad would be given the written mandate. Before this time, the knights hoped it would be possible to rescue Jobyna from the King's Castle. Luke was thankful for this provision and was greatly encouraged as plans for the rescue were made.

As soon as Jobyna was able to sit up unaided, the nurse, with her most satisfactory monetary reward, returned to the city. She was pleased and surprised how quickly the girl was recovering. The woman took credit for this, but she secretly knew Jobyna was strong-willed and a survivor. Jobyna was told the servant women would continue to care for her under the direction of a special doctor. When she was well enough to talk, she would be presented to King Elliad and she must begin to think about the things he might ask her. The woman who fed Jobyna and cared for her the day the nurse left was sullen and silent. Jobyna had the definite feeling this woman held resentment and dislike toward her.

Later in the morning, two men came into the room. Jobyna recognized one of them. She had heard him addressed as "Doctor Gilbert." He was the one in charge of mixing her medicine.

Of a slight build, Doctor Gilbert's straight brown hair was streaked with gray. The sadness haunting his light brown eyes was accentuated by the marked down-turn at each corner.

"Jobyna," the doctor told her, "this is John, a doctor from Samdene. King Elliad has appointed him to take care of you. You are to do as he says so you will soon be well."

Jobyna scrutinized the new doctor, John. She remembered her father's friend, and King Leopold's counselor, Sir Samuel, who was from Samdene. Though much younger, this man, John, reminded her of Samuel. It was the piercing blue eyes and thick eyebrows that sparked the resemblance. John had soft brown hair and his vivid blue eyes were accentuated by suntanned skin. His eyes seemed to look into her very soul. Jobyna lowered her eyes and her head. She remembered the stream. No, she wouldn't fight the current; the flow of her life was taking her on further to recovery and eventually to a meeting with Elliad.

Doctor John left the care of Jobyna to the women, but he was always present to administer her medicine and feed her at meal times. She was able to consume a little bread dipped in broth, and when John brought each spoonful to her mouth, his blue eyes meeting hers made Jobyna feel hot and uncomfortable.

"This morning, we will see if you can stand," John ordered. Gilbert cast a dubious look, but nevertheless came to take Jobyna's other arm when John lifted her out of the bed. Jobyna surprised them all; she walked across the room. When the men left her to walk unaided, her steps were a little wobbly yet she continued on, encouraged by the look of pleasure radiating from John's eyes.

Jobyna's progress was amazing. John was pleased with her improvement. When the sun finally peeped out from behind the clouds for a while, he put a woolen cloak and thick rug around her, opened the doors, picked her up in his strong arms, carried her down a long corridor and out on to the battlement. Soldiers on guard shifted uneasily as John walked past carrying Jobyna. She was little more than a featherweight to the strong man.

The battlement faced the city; the view was indeed breathtaking. Fresh spring air brought a faint glow of apple blossom color to Jobyna's cheeks and John saw her smile for the first time. With his arm around her back for support, she sat on the great parapet.

"How wonderful," she whispered.

"You spoke!" John's voice was ecstatic. This was real headway.

Jobyna was absorbed with looking past the turrets and towers, out beyond the castle walls, across the gray stone city toward a row of mountainous cliffs. She knew just over the ridge there lay her special valley.

John followed her gaze, noticing the concentration on her face. "Jobyna," he said, "speak to me again."

She opened her mouth and again the faint husky whisper came, "What do you want me to say?"

"Anything you like," he encouraged her.

She laughed a croaking laugh, the small exertion making her cough. Jobyna broke into a severe coughing fit, each cough racking her body with such violence that she retched with each gasp. She clung to John for support; he held her close to his chest and stroked her hair as she struggled for each breath. The sun was gone and the small patch of blue was quickly filling up with ominous black clouds. Suddenly the wind whistled up, jerking the cloak from Jobyna's knees. John pulled the rug up over the girl's head and carried her back along the silent corridor to the familiar room. The two women helped Jobyna back to bed while John brought her more medicine.

"Do I have to?" she croaked, pulling a face and poking out her tongue. The women looked up in surprise at the sound of the patient's new found voice.

John nodded at them. "Yes, Jobyna has found her voice at last."

As though by cue, the two women retreated from the room. Gilbert spoke to John, with a gentle warning in his tone. "We will have to be careful that she does not strain herself, John, and wear herself out." Gilbert knew the man was pushing his patient as hard as he could. He too left the room.

"Jobyna," John's voice sounded sad, "you know I have my orders, don't you?" She nodded as she looked into his serious eyes. "King Elliad wants you to be happy and to live a long and fulfilled life," he lied. "There are certain things he wants to know from you. He has told me I must have answers from you for certain questions."

Jobyna looked at John with unbelieving eyes. "Why doesn't he come and see me himself?"

John's eyes never moved off hers. "He is afraid you would be frightened and would not talk to him."

Jobyna tried to speak, but the effort turned to another coughing fit. John rose, crossed to the small table and returned with some fruit juice. He held the goblet to the captive's lips while she sipped it. She slowly savored the nectar's soothing sweetness. His gaze made her feel uneasy; her heart beat faster.

"Jobyna, where is the Seal to the Kingdom of Frencolia?" John asked her.

Jobyna looked at him, incredulity in her eyes. "How do you know about the seal?" she queried, her soft husky voice sounding tired.

"I have seen King Leopold's last testament." John was choosing his words carefully. His face showed extreme self-control. Jobyna believed now for sure King Elliad had especially appointed John to get information from her. She sighed, exhausted, and lay back on the cushions.

"Do you know where your brother Luke is?" John asked her persistently.

"No." Jobyna shook her head, asking impertinently, "Do you?"

His blue eyes glared into hers. "If I were to tell you that King Elliad is going to kill me if I don't get the information from you, how would you feel?" he asked her.

Jobyna looked away from him. "Very sad," she replied, her large green eyes filling with tears.

John left the room. The women returned and Jobyna fell into a restless sleep for a short while.

Early in the evening, John entered the room with her meal, hot lamb stew.

"I can easily feed myself." Jobyna stated as John drew a chair up by the bed.

"Yes, I'm sure you can," he told her, "but I have strict instructions to see you get proper nourishment. I must do my job, or . . . " and John drew his forefinger across his throat, smiling. Jobyna grimaced and pulled a face at him. They were alone in the room so Jobyna dared to ask, "What did Elliad say when you told him I would not tell you anything?"

"Do you really want to know?" John said as he spooned the stew to her. She chewed a little, then swallowed.

"What does Elliad look like?" Jobyna asked.

John filled her mouth again. He did not answer this time. Jobyna swallowed, emptying her mouth. "Luke says he has dark hair and a brown beard. He said Elliad makes him think of what the devil would look like."

John laughed long and hard at this outburst. "And you wouldn't think I looked at all like the devil, Jobyna, daughter of Chanec?"

"Oh, no." Jobyna answered seriously. "You're more like an angel!"

John chuckled loudly. When Jobyna could eat no more, John fetched a comb from the mantelpiece and began combing her hair, taking special care with the knots; he did not want to hurt her tender scalp. While completing this exercise, he asked her, "When are you going to tell me what King Elliad wants to know?"

Jobyna waited until he had finished combing her hair and replied, "I feel I should speak to him myself, John. It is not fair that he is using you in this way. No one's life should be at stake but mine! You can tell him I am prepared to see him. That is why I wanted to come here."

John looked up sharply, "You wanted to come here, Jobyna?"

"Yes. In actual fact, I gave myself up." John was not looking at her, his mind elsewhere. He rose thoughtfully.

"John, I'm tired of sitting in bed in this nightgown. I want you to bring me my clothes so I can walk a little. I will get stronger and I can go and see Elliad."

John took her hand between his two. A chill ran through her body which he, in turn, felt. "Jobyna," he said, looking at her face but not quite meeting her eyes, "I wish you would confide in me. It would help both you and me a lot."

"You must be very afraid of Elliad." Jobyna said sadly. "John, have you seen anyone die?"

John looked up at this sudden change in subject. "Many times," he answered truthfully.

"I don't mean as a doctor, but have you seen someone . . . killed?"

John was frustrated with this conversation; it was going nowhere. His whole face changed to that of disdain. Dropping her hand, he said, "I will tell King Elliad what you have asked and see if I can get an audience for you." Turning on his heel, he left the room. John did not return that day. Gilbert gave Jobyna her medicine that night making her feel ill at ease, out of routine.

Elliad's anger was kindled, his operation "Gentle John" was not working as quickly as he had expected. John was getting nowhere fast. So, the girl wanted to see him herself did she? That was interesting. She was a lot stronger willed than he first imagined. Elliad ordered a daygown to be sent for Jobyna and increased the watch in the area of her room. It would not do for her to go wandering around. The castle was a tremendous size with many hiding places. She had recovered much faster than anticipated. The doctors informed him that in certain cases the progress she had made would take many weeks. Her constitution must be strong for that of a woman!

John took the gown with him in the morning. He gave the girl her medicine, then fed her the breakfast. He seemed agitated, Jobyna worried as to the reason why he would show such an attitude.

The sound of soldiers' footsteps echoed from the corridor. The marching came closer and closer. Gilbert entered the room. John rose instinctively and turned toward the doctor. "There's an urgent message for you . . . " John hushed the older man in mid-sentence and left the room, closing the door behind him. Jobyna waited for John's return; this was not forthcoming and she was sure the soldiers had taken him away.

Jobyna fingered the new gown. It was made of finely woven wool, a delicate pale blue. Silver thread was sewn into the sleeves and hem. The women helped Jobyna dress, and combed her hair. Gilbert, sensing Jobyna's preoccupation, said she could walk about the corridor but she must not venture to the battlement if it was raining. She was to check with Gilbert before

114

going outside. Jobyna felt John's absence at lunch time. Food was brought to the table in her room and she fed herself. There were no smiles or words of encouragement. Silent as usual, the women stood watching, always watching.

Gilbert paced up and down; he seemed agitated. Opening the shutters, he turned to Jobyna and said, "The rain has stopped, Jobyna, you may put on the cloak here and go out in the fresh air after you've eaten."

Gilbert accompanied Jobyna to the battlements. The air was fresh and the smell of rain hung in the misty damp. The cliffs were draped with gray clouds swirling around the jagged tops. Jobyna could see a company of soldiers and knights on horseback, going out across one of the drawbridges. She thought of her own capture and memories came flooding back. Gilbert uttered an exclamation and at the same time she recognized John, riding in the middle of the soldiers. *Why, there were 40 or 50 horses.*

"John," she called out, but her strained cry was lost in the wind. Gilbert drew her away from the parapet. "Where are they taking him?" she cried.

Gilbert took Jobyna's arm and ushered her back inside. He was sorry he had taken her out; he should have known better. King Elliad would be upset with him and to stir the king's anger was worth more than one's life!

Jobyna paced up and down, up and down. Gilbert had gone out, leaving one of the women with her. Her guardian was the sullen-faced woman who glowered silently at Jobyna when the girl spoke or asked a question. Jobyna asked her name, but the woman just glared and did not answer.

The captive was permitted to walk the corridor, but when she came to a corner, two soldiers stepped out and barred her way. There were two soldiers posted in every doorway and all she could do was turn on her heel, walk back to her room and start again. She paced until her legs ached, then returned to her room for a nap. Curling up on the cushions on the bed, she drew a rug over her feet. Thoughts of John bothered her greatly. She was worried for this disturbingly blue-eyed Doctor John! She cared about him!

Jobyna awoke from her nap hot and perspiring. The wool dress was damp and clingy. She decided to return to the corridor. Gilbert strode from the far corner as she paced back and forth.

"Jobyna, you're flushed," he put his hand on her forehead. "You're burning up. How long have you been this way?" He guided her back to the room and took a bottle off the shelf. Pouring a small amount of thick syrup into a tiny thimble-sized pottery container, he told her to drink it, and rest. Jobyna complied but the fever persisted and Gilbert stirred some powder into a goblet of fruit juice and told her drink it all. She fell into a listless sleep.

When Jobyna awoke this time, the room was in darkness. She could barely make out Gilbert's form. He had food for her. Sitting up, she noted the two women present, one of them lighting the lamps.

"Where is John?" Jobyna inquired. "Is he back yet?" The questions remained unanswered. "Gilbert, would Elliad really kill John?" Jobyna did not miss the looks that passed between the three and she felt sure her worst fears were true. Gilbert did not answer. "I must see this Elliad. If he wants to kill someone, then it should be me! Why didn't he just let me die?"

Jobyna could not settle into sleep that night; she tossed and turned. In the past week her world had become one small room and the people in it important to her. Every time she closed her eyes she saw John's blue ones, staring at her in his uncanny way. Gilbert finally gave her an extra draft, sponging the perspiration from her face. He dispatched a message to Elliad informing him the girl was heading for a relapse, but word came back that the king had gone on a mission and may not return until the morning.

Jobyna experienced another nightmare. She saw hundreds of soldiers in the valley, her valley. Elliad was there. She knew him by the purple hood he wore over his face. They were chasing after John. She wanted to take him into the treasure cave to hide but the wall was unmovable and they were trapped. The soldiers entered the outer cave and she cried out as they drew their swords. She stood between them and John, but they pushed her out of the way. She watched as John's body was cut into hundreds of pieces. Even in her nightmare she could see the bright color of blood. Blood splattered the walls and dribbled to the stone floor. Red splashed on her face and her hands were covered in the sticky scarlet liquid. Yet through the crimson his blue eyes were still looking at her and she could see the horror of death on his face. Jobyna woke up screaming and crying. Gilbert and the women had to restrain her to keep her in bed.

11

Luke and Sabin were no longer at the Knight's Tower at Mayhew. The newly declared king had been secretly moved to the northern border of the kingdom, beyond Leroy—the town where Sir Dorai was duke—to a Border Castle. A Border Castle was even more impenetrable than a Knight's Tower. It was twice the size with twice the security.

Luke felt sad to be moving further away from his sister, but realized he had no choice but to comply. The senior knights did not want him near the front lines when they sent Elliad the mandate. The men considered Luke's relocation as part of taking care of Frencolia. Sir Dorai arranged for news to be relayed to Luke as it came to hand. The Border Castle was posted with over 200 knights and soldiers to guard the newly appointed King Luke Chanec.

Elliad, while out on his information-gathering mission, was led to believe that Luke Chanec was holding a whole Knight's Tower captive. This seemed incredible and highly ridiculous to him and he rode over to Mayhew to investigate. The suspicions were confirmed; Mayhew Knight's Tower was in a state of siege. Soldiers were on guard at the gates and he spied longbows at the ready. A Knight's Tower was impregnable. He would have to retreat, gather reinforcements and make plans. It seemed inconceivable that Luke, a mere boy, could overthrow a Knight's Tower! This new development worried him greatly as he rode back to the city. *How could a boy capture practically a whole army? How many men did he have? How many Knights were involved? What right did Luke have to be doing this?*

"Halt, who goes there?" A powerfully deep voice rang out as Elliad's company rounded a bend. It was after sunset and the descending darkness and rising mist made it difficult to see. The sound of swords sliding from their sheaths pervaded the still night air.

One of Elliad's knights called out, "Your King, Elliad! Put your swords down and make way!"

The deep voice reverberated once more, "Forget the others, go for Elliad."

The attacking men called out, "For Frencolia!" The next half-hour was filled with the confusion of a battle on horseback in almost dark conditions.

Elliad's knights stayed near their king, trying to cut a path through the mass of horses and men. Oaths and curses rang out as the dusk made it very difficult for a man to see his enemy. The air was thick with the smell of death. Swords found their mark as men tumbled to the ground and were trampled under hoof. Groans of dying men soon made it obvious that skilled swordsmen were among the attackers.

"Sire, there are too many of them. We'd best try to work our way past and get to the city," Berg, the king's chief bodyguard, declared over the commotion. Elliad could see there was sense in this. He could not tell which men were on which side and wondered if the men knew themselves! Berg, riding next to Elliad, uttered a guttural yell, leaned over and gathered the reigns of Elliad's horse.

Without regard for his own life, he spurred the horses on through the mass, his sword arm slashing fervently at the obstructions directly in front of them. Elliad's sword arm too swung with haste; slash, stab, drive, like a maniacal machine. Elliad's strength began to wane. He lurched, unsteady in the saddle. Righting himself he realized he was galloping toward the castle and safety, with a dozen of his men. Sheathing his sword, he noted his arm was soaked with blood to the elbow, though he had not incurred as much as a scratch. He ordered his men to investigate the scene of ambush in the morning.

Officials at the castle met him when he arrived, explaining two pressing matters: there was a group of six Frencolian knights to see him, and the girl Jobyna had suffered a relapse. Elliad, still rather shaken by the attempt made on his life just half a mile outside the city gates, decided he would see the knights first.

The six knights were brought to Elliad in the throne room. He recognized Ruskin, who was acting as the knights' spokesman. Ruskin told Elliad he had secret information for him, and asked what it was worth?

Elliad sneered at this, "What is it worth? How would I know? I could get it out of you in other ways though if you wish."

Ruskin moved uneasily. "How would you feel if I told you that Luke, Son of Chanec, is wearing the Seal to the Kingdom of Frencolia?"

"And how would you feel if I told you I already knew this?" Elliad lied smugly, knowing he had the upper hand.

Ruskin knelt before him once more. "Sire," he

said, "we are concerned that Frencolia may fall into the hands of a novice, a boy. Some of the knights believe that Luke Chanec should be king instead of you. Sire, we are here to protect your rights to the throne of the kingdom." The other knights nodded their agreement. Elliad sat back. This was a boost for his pride. He glanced from one to the other and was inclined to give them more than the benefit of the doubt.

Ruskin continued, "We risked our lives to come tonight, sire. The company was divided and we had to fight our way through them."

Elliad knew from his own experience that this was feasible. "Tell me what you know," Elliad commanded and listened intently as Ruskin explained the situation. Luke was in possession of the Knight's Tower at Mayhew and some knights there were acting in protection of him. He asked Ruskin for names and was not surprised to hear Sir Dorai's. He accepted Ruskin when the knight produced a drawing of the seal and explained what it looked like in great detail. Elliad was well aware of the power invested in the wearing of the seal. If only he could get his hands on it!

"The senior knights are trying to gather all the able men of the country together and plan to pronounce Luke Chanec, King of Frencolia," Ruskin explained.

Elliad called in his own counselors and knights and the discussion went on deep into the night. They believed Luke was more interested in protecting himself than in actually coming out in aggression. What more could one expect of a boy? Elliad's mind went to the sister. Maybe she could be used to bait him a little. He entertained the thought briefly. Jobyna bothered him and he was deeply troubled. Then the seeds of a new plan for his captive began to germinate in his mind. He remembered the news of her relapse and decided in spite of the late hour, he would have John visit her—it may prove interesting.

Jobyna dreamed the same dream about John's execution and woke up for a second time in great distress. She sat up, crying and shaking.

The door swung open and there stood—John.

"John, oh, John!" Jobyna cried, her voice showing great relief. John stared at Jobyna. Her eyes were glazed and her face flushed. Her long brown hair was wild and tangled. Great sobs shook her frame uncontrollably. John was speechless. He took a chair to her bedside, telling the women and Gilbert to leave.

"I dreamed Elliad killed you, like you said he might. It was horrible."

Gilbert spoke up, "John." John did not look at

him. "John, let me talk with you." Gilbert went and stood at the door, waiting.

John ignored him and spoke to Jobyna, "Tell me about it, Jobyna." Gilbert shut the door. They were alone.

Jobyna told him about her nightmare. He listened silently as she unfolded the gory picture. She was trembling and feverish. He took her small hand, his eyes gleaming with triumph.

"But you're here," she said finally.

"Jobyna, this valley, is it a real place?" he asked.

"Oh, yes, it's beautiful. . . ." Her voice trailed off.

"And the treasure cave, too?"

She stared at him, realizing now what she had told him. She did not answer, but her look told John all he wanted to know.

"You know how to get inside this cave, don't you Jobyna?" His voice held a threatening note. "Is the seal inside the cave, Jobyna?"

Jobyna began shaking and crying. "No," she told him, "Luke put the seal around his neck and he can't get it off. It belongs to King Leopold . . . and . . . King Leopold is in the cave, dead."

"What else did you find in the cave, Jobyna?" John's voice was soft and imploring.

"Luke opened chests of gold coins and there were jewels of all sorts. There were clothes and . . . " Jobyna's voice trailed off. She was exhausted and the drugs in her system were taking effect.

"How many chests full of treasure were there Jobyna?" John asked persistently, shaking her shoulder gently.

"Oh, they were everywhere, heaps . . . of . . . them . . . " Her voice faded and with eyes closed, she said, "But John's all right . . . Elliad didn't kill him. . . . "

John knew he had achieved more than he thought possible that night. He would not stop now, he must keep questioning her. He needed to think. He dare not spoil it by saying the wrong thing. How could he get her to tell him the way into the cave? He paced to the fireplace and back again. The girl slumped back on the cushions, the second draft of sedative taking over her body.

"Jobyna." He shook her hard, slapping her face, but it was no use. He opened the door and beckoned to Gilbert. "Keep her drugged, I'll be back later," he said as he strode off along the corridor.

Gilbert sat up dozing off and on, watching Jobyna in between his naps. She slept extremely well, and there was no need to give her more drugs as suggested. Her fever subsided.

In the morning Jobyna was much better. She asked for John. Gilbert gruffly said he was busy with other things. Jobyna remembered him coming last night and knew she had divulged something about the treasures in the cave. John had questioned her and for some reason she had told him, but her mind was hazy as to what was real and what was just dreams. The girl began to wonder if there was something sinister about John and felt she needed to be careful.

It was noon when John finally arrived. Jobyna completed consuming hot broth. He sat down at the table opposite her. As before, everyone left the room. John's normally broad shoulders were stooped in worry.

"Something is wrong, isn't it, John?" Jobyna asked.

This was John's cue, "Yes, Jobyna. There is news of Luke."

Jobyna sat up straight. "Luke, what of Luke?"

John told Jobyna King Elliad had taken Luke as his prisoner and was holding him in the Knight's Tower at Mayhew. The look on John's face made Jobyna wonder if he was telling the truth. John said, "King Elliad will release Luke if you tell him where the treasure cave is and how to get to it."

"You're lying!" Jobyna exclaimed with sarcasm in her voice, shaking her head. Jobyna's forthrightness shocked John and his blue eyes grew dark. He frowned, working hard to contain his feelings. "Let me go to Elliad, and let him tell me these things himself." She looked at John in a new light. "Who are you, anyway?" she accused. "What are you? I don't think you're a doctor!" John's face softened. He laughed a scoffing laugh. She continued, "If it is true, and Elliad has got Luke, then how do I know he will let him go free? What I know of him, he would kill us both and have the treasure, too."

"I have someone who can tell you the truth, Jobyna." He walked to the door and opened it. "Come in, Ruskin," he said.

Jobyna tried to meet Ruskin's eyes, but he would not look at her. John stood between them for a moment and then closed the door.

"Is it true, Ruskin? Has Elliad really got Luke as his prisoner?" Jobyna cried, taking his hand, trying to get him to look at her. Ruskin stared at John and John returned the gaze.

"Yes, it is true. If you want Luke to live, then you must do everything King Elliad says." Ruskin turned to the table. "Let us sit down and discuss this, Jobyna."

Jobyna was trembling. She stood her ground. "I don't believe you," she cried. "There is something missing. Why haven't I seen Elliad?" Ruskin and John were silent. "How do I know Luke is still alive? How do I know Elliad hasn't killed him?"

She walked across to the shuttered window. Composing herself, she turned to them saying,

"You're both traitors. I know you're acting. I could have trusted you, John, but you do not have any truth in your heart, only your own interest. I don't know what I am to you and I hope Elliad is giving you a big reward for your efforts to get information out of me." In bitterness she turned to include Ruskin, "Neither of you care for Frencolia or anyone in it, only for your own skins. I would rather die than betray my country. Why don't you take me to Elliad and get it over with?"

John strode to the table and banged his clenched fist down hard upon the wooden top. The utensils leaped with the force of the movement. He struggled to control himself. Turning on Jobyna, he shouted with anger thick in his voice, "So you'd rather die than talk, would you?" His blue eyes looked deep into hers and she saw for the first time a glimpse of the monster he was. His game was almost over. "You will get your wish, Jobyna, daughter of Chanec of Chanoine. You will see your Elliad when he is ready; he will grant you your desire to die!"

12

Sabin matched his stride to Luke's as they paced the floor together. With one day left before the deadline, the two realized that it was an impossible task to rescue Jobyna from Elliad. Guarded every minute of the day and night, the area of the castle where she was being held was crawling with soldiers. It had been Luke's idea to have Ruskin and the five other knights pretend to support Elliad. A little truth would go a long way in making Elliad believe their story. Sir Dorai elaborated on the idea and Ruskin was pleased to be able to serve Luke and Frencolia in this way. The charade was dangerous, but they were sure Elliad would fall for it. A drawing of the seal was to be sacrificed to substantiate the story.

Luke felt much happier to know Ruskin was present in the castle, even though grossly outnumbered by the enemy. He prayed Ruskin would gain support and help from others in the castle, but it was obvious the plan was treacherous. The knights reluctantly agreed that the mandate had to be delivered when the deadline was up in the morning. The boy tossed and turned sleeplessly, remembering his sister's more carefree days. He remembered her words to him as they rode for the last time from their home in Chanoine: "If we die, we live. And if we live, we will die one day and then live. There is nothing to lose."

Luke knew his loss would be great if she were to die.

The sun rose on a rain-soaked King's Castle, making the battlements shine black as though polished. Jobyna strolled back and forth on the battlement walk, carefully watched by four soldiers. The hood of the cloak was pulled over her head. No one else walked with her. Her cough was bothering her and she felt tired. A bad premonition about this new day nagged at her mind, and she tried to dismiss it as her own silly anxiety. Lifting her eyes to the sun, rising over the clifftops, she tried to think of something other than her situation. There was movement from the soldiers as the guard was changed.

Jobyna edged near the parapet as one of the soldiers going off duty marched past. She did not want to be in his way and hinder his movement at all. The soldier jostled her and she almost fell on to the walk. He caught her by the hand, saying, "Get out of my way, woman!" She felt a piece of paper being pressed into her palm.

Her heart pounded as she carefully unfolded the note. Jobyna leaned on the great ledge of the parapet between the stone battlements. She listened for footsteps and lifted the bottom of the note, so the sun would catch the writing, making it easier to read. There was a tiny drawing of the seal in the corner and Jobyna's heart began to race.

"Do not be afraid, you have friends in the castle. A rescue is being planned for you. Be prepared. Luke is safe. May God be with you. K.F. Destroy this note."

Jobyna ran her eyes over the words again. Could she believe such a note? A voice behind her made her start in fright. In her moment of intense concentration, John had silently crept up on her. "What has the little sparrow got—a piece of bread?" With one arm, John pinned her arms to her sides and with the other he reached around her, plucking the note from her fingers. He held her tight while he read it.

"Where did you get this?" John turned her to face him and with his hand on her throat pushed her back against the hard stone wall.

"So it is true, Luke is safe. There are people in this castle who do care about Frencolia!" Jobyna gasped these words out as John's fingers dug into her throat and jaw bone.

In contempt John turned and with one swing of his muscular arm, he threw Jobyna down on the stone walk. "You're dead!" he muttered as he strode off along the battlement.

Jobyna limped back to the room, her hip aching from the jarring it received in her fall. Thankfully her injury was only momentary and the pain ceased after a few minutes. The morning dragged on for Jobyna as she sat in her room, contemplating her situation.

Elliad was furious with the note! It confirmed his suspicions that there was treachery going on among those who were closest to him. He called all his K.E. knights and all other officials and counselors to a meeting in the throne room. He told them the situation and explained that any of them could leave if they wished, he only wanted men who were loyal first to him, then to Frencolia. Those who showed true loyalty would be given honor and promotion. He gave them one hour to decide what they would do. Elliad ordered double guard to be posted at all exits and no one was to enter or leave without good reason. He himself would have trusted personal bodyguards with him at all times. Anyone approaching him in a suspicious way would be dealt with on the spot.

"I want provisions made for this castle to assume a state of siege. We will maintain this stronghold and soon gain control of the country. The girl Jobyna knows the way to King Leopold's vast treasure chamber and when we find this treasure, there will be a share for all who remain loyal. Any sign of disloyalty will be dealt with by instant death!" Elliad outlined other plans and details of the siege, then called his closest counselors to meet him in the conference room in one hour.

Jobyna was oblivious to what took place outside her confined space but she knew there was no help found in worry. Help would come from prayer. Ignoring the others in the room, Jobyna knelt by a chair and poured out her heart to God. The rustling of paper did not stop her prayer, but a hand pulling roughly on her arm brought her back to her predicament.

"Get up!" John shouted.

When Jobyna stood and turned around, she was alone with John and a K.E. knight. There were papers on the table. John spoke. "First, we have some documents here we want you to sign." His voice was wooden, with no emotion. "If you don't sign them, then my friend, Berg here, will break your fingers one by one. After that, you will tell us how to get to the treasure cave."

Jobyna drew in a sharp breath, looking up at John. She started to cough uncontrollably. He brought her a drink. Sipping it, she cleared her throat. Her trembling hand reached for one of the papers. The accusations in the document brought tears to her eyes.

"You want me to sign this confession stating I was responsible for poisoning King Leopold, with the help of Luke?" The men were silent as Jobyna read on. "I tried to kill King Elliad? I incited Luke to work against the country of Frencolia and helped him raise an army?" She laughed in amazement and shock, shaking her head. "I won't sign this." She put the paper down on the table. "You will use it anyway, but for me to sign it would be to lie against God and my country." She looked into John's face. "You know these accusations are lies, John."

John looked through her. She would never

forget the empty expression in his blue eyes. His hands were brutal as he held her shoulders! Berg forced her left hand on to the table. One of the knight's large hands pinned it down at the wrist and held it fast. Flexing the strong thumb and forefinger of his other hand, Berg grasped the joint of her first finger. In one flowing motion he jerked the finger backwards toward her elbow, twisting the joint until it uttered a popping sound. Jobyna screamed in pain. She tried to get up, but John held her down securely. She was aware that this was not a nightmare and the excruciating pain in her hand was real.

"You . . . enjoy this . . . don't you?" she said between gasps of pain.

"Immensely!" John returned. "You do far too much chirping, Sparrow! Later on we will have your tongue!" He held the pen close to her face and pushed the ink bottle toward her. "You have nine more chances, Jobyna, sister of Luke Chanec the traitor."

Jobyna knew John was deadly earnest. He would have this monster break all her fingers while he held her. These were the kind of men Elliad enjoyed the company of! "We do not have all day, Sparrow! I will count to 10. If you do not sign, then we will clip another of your wings!" He began counting. "One . . . two . . . three . . . "

A knight entered the room and John spun

around. "How dare you come in here. I gave strict orders . . . "

"Sir, you must come! There is a very urgent document from the Knight's Tower at Mayhew. We could not wait. Do you want to take it here, sir?" His eyes were on Jobyna, who was sobbing in extreme anguish, cradling her hand to her breast.

John let out an exasperated sigh. "Bring the documents!" he snapped at Berg, who hastily collected them.

Jobyna was left alone. She sat swaying back and forth, her eyes closed. Sharp pains shooting up her arm were paramount. The door opened and Gilbert entered. Great sadness in his brown eyes deepened as he saw her deformed hand.

Gilbert prepared Jobyna some medicine, saying, "It will help the pain." Then he gently laid her hand on the table. "This will hurt," he warned, "but I must do it." He leaned across in front of her so she could not see what he was doing. Gilbert expertly pulled the joints back into place, manipulating and stretching her finger and hand. She cried loudly, for it hurt more than anything she had experienced before. He gathered a bandage from the cupboard and bound her fingers tightly together.

"There are some things you must know, Jobyna." Gilbert spoke softly and quickly as he secured the bandage firmly around her hand. "There are many men in this castle who are not

137

loyal to King Elliad. There have been plans to rescue you but King Elliad has made it too difficult. His constant presence with you has made it impossible."

Jobyna could not comprehend this. "What do you mean, Gilbert? Elliad has not been here."

Gilbert glanced back at the closed door. "Jobyna, Elliad *is* John!" He saw shocked disbelief in her eyes. "John is Elliad! They are the same person. Elliad did not think you would talk to him as King Elliad, so he shaved off his beard and invented John. Everyone was forced to go along with his ridiculous pretence."

Jobyna felt sick and angry. The pain in her hand seemed nothing compared to this knowledge, this torture to her mind. It made her realize the lengths to which Elliad would go to achieve his ends. Waves of embarrassment and remorse swamped the girl as she remembered she almost trusted him as a friend. She had called him an "angel." Some angel he turned out to be!

Gilbert's voice brought her back from her thoughts. Realizing her shocked state, the doctor repeated his warning several times. "Jobyna, you must not let Elliad know what I have said here. He will guess someone has told you for he is sure you will not work it out yourself. You must treat him as John. Elliad has an incredible intuition to guess what people are thinking. He must believe he still has you fooled. Our lives depend on it at this moment!

If he does reveal himself to you as Elliad, you must act surprised . . . Jobyna!"

Jobyna nodded numbly. She said, despairingly, "What chance do we have against such a violent, evil man? He is devoid of any goodness!" At a loss to imagine what would happen next, the girl was thankful of Gilbert's presence with her. He talked in undertones for the rest of the morning and told her what was happening in the kingdom. Word had circulated through the knights and soldiers that Luke was wearing the Seal to the Kingdom of Frencolia and had been pronounced king by the lords and senior knights.

Gilbert told Jobyna he had heard messages being passed in the castle by those loyal to Luke. The number of men turning against Elliad was growing every hour. The castle was full of people loyal to Luke. Some of them had even left to join the army being gathered in support of Luke. Gilbert informed Jobyna that he did not think Elliad was aware just how many were no longer loyal to him. She must be ready to be rescued at any moment.

"How could I have thought of John as a friend? How easily deceived I am."

"You have been very ill," Gilbert said, greatly agitated. "In fact, we were sure you would die. Elliad acted kind and concerned, and in your weak state, you had no choice but to accept him as a friend." He leaned back in his chair. "Yes, Elliad is a very good actor, and a very vicious operator." He sighed a sigh of extreme helplessness.

Elliad John paced back and forth across the throne room. His trusted knights and counselors were in the room, all talking at once. There was a great commotion! The mandate had been read in their presence. He sat on the throne and his eyes narrowed as he looked at the men. Who could he really trust? When one cannot be trusted oneself, it is hard to find another man in whom to place confidence. He must keep control of Frencolia! This country was his! It must not go to the boy, Luke!

13

Luke rode a horse around the small garden and courtyard at the Border Castle. There were tender vegetable plants sprouting and he was careful to keep to the paths lest the hooves squash the tender foliage. He looked up as he heard the side drawbridge being lowered over the moat. Two knights waited on the other side ready to cross.

News, he thought. Leading the horse back to the stable, he waited for the men. Following the knights through the hall, he entered the office where Sir Valdre was waiting. Sir Dorai, who had stayed at the Knight's Tower at Mayhew, had sent information. As usual, the senior knight read the communication to himself first.

It was a lengthy message, and there were several pages in the pouch. He ordered the messengers to wait at the door. Luke waited, watching Sir Valdre's face, trying to be patient. The moments passed slowly. Valdre was deep in thought for a while after he studied the papers. Luke knew he would not hide anything from him and the silence made him apprehensive.

"Elliad has answered the mandate he received yesterday with a statement of his own. He says he cannot accept the mandate and believes Luke Chanec has lied to the lords and senior knights, bewitching them with the stolen seal. He is saddened by such treachery and hopes the loyal men of Frencolia will see this deception. He has accused you, Your Majesty, and your sister, of conspiring together against the kingdom of Frencolia. He states, and of course we know this to be false, that Jobyna Chanec has confessed to poisoning King Leopold and that your father and you helped her to hide his body in a secret cave."

Luke's face was a mixture of emotions. Valdre continued, "Elliad wants you to surrender to him so that there can be peace restored to Frencolia and King Leopold can be given the state funeral he deserves." Luke opened his mouth to speak. Valdre hushed him with a raised hand, "There is more, Luke. He says . . . " The knight turned the paper towards Luke. "Read it for yourself. . . . "

Luke was aware of great emotion on Valdre's face. He took the document and read the passage indicated to him. "If Luke, Son of Chanec of Chanoine does not surrender by the end of the week, then Jobyna, Daughter of Chanec of Chanoine, will be executed for her treason against the country and throne." The decree was signed "King Elliad John Pruwitt, King of Frencolia." Luke felt numb. He stared blankly at the tapestry on the far wall.

Accompanying papers gave details of other plans being carried out around the country. Luke had a hard time keeping his mind on Valdre's conversation. Sir Valdre was well aware of the trauma Luke was suffering but knew they must face the truth. Valdre explained how foot-soldiers were being organized into companies, each knight responsible for 100 men in units of 10, captained by soldiers on horseback.

Men of every walk of life had signed up in support of Luke. The new enlistments were sick and tired of a reign of terror and bloodshed governed by Elliad. The country was preparing to do battle. There was no talk of Luke surrendering and the boy-king knew this was completely out of the question. Elliad would kill him and all those loyal to Frencolia and carry on in his depraved ways. All towns, castles and towers in the country were being prepared for siege so Elliad would have no where to go ir Frencolia if he left the King's

Castle. Valdre was somewhat concerned that Elliad's statements about King Leopold's poisoning would be believed by some, but he knew Sir Dorai would take care of this with a counter-statement. He was correct in his assumption.

Jobyna had been moved three times that day. Once she was taken to a tower on the battlements; another time to a dungeon down under the castle, and finally back to her original room. A large number of soldiers accompanied each move. She guessed the maneuvers would confuse those who may be trying to rescue her. Elliad must be worried to go to such lengths. She was dreading another meeting with the tyrant. In pain and suffering, she was not sure what she would tell "John." She was relieved when Gilbert entered the room. He brought food and drink for her as she had eaten nothing all day. A soldier entered the room with Gilbert and stood in front of the door.

"How do you fare, girl?" Gilbert's voice was harsh.

Jobyna supposed this was for the sake of the soldier. "I am well, but my hand is very painful today. It has been throbbing and throbbing."

Gilbert unwrapped it, and examined the

bruised, swollen mass. "I will return soon. Eat your meal." Gilbert left the room, followed by the soldier who remained outside. She ate what she could of the bread and cheese and enjoyed the flask of milk.

The doctor returned and this time the soldier did not come in the room. Gilbert had told him he needed privacy or the girl would not talk to him. He spoke urgently to her, rubbing her hand with a pungent ointment. She winced.

"If you are approached by someone, Jobyna, who asks you to go with them, whether it be a soldier, a woman—anyone—then be sure to go. A rescue is being planned, even if you can only be hidden somewhere in the castle, out of Elliad's clutches." Gilbert sighed, "I wish I knew of such a place. . . . "

Jobyna decided it was time to tell Gilbert about the secret passages. "Gilbert, when Luke and I were in the cave where King Leopold's body lies, we found some charts and maps showing secret passages which go under the castle and between the walls. If I could only get into the throne room. Some of the dungeons have secret exits but it would be hard to know which dungeon is which, there are so many. The way to trigger the opening of the secret entrances is very complicated. They took me down to a dungeon today but I lost my sense of direction after going down so many stairs. I found the symbols hard to work out on the maps of the dungeons. I did understand the way out of the throne room, though. It joins up with other passages."

Gilbert had opened a bag of bandages, ointments and potions. He took her injured hand gently in his and said to her, "Jobyna, what I am going to do now will hurt, but for the healing of your hand, it must be done." She looked into his sad eyes. They were the saddest eyes she had ever seen. "I am a doctor first, Jobyna, and I have always worked to save life, to heal and to cure. You'll always remember that, won't you?" She nodded.

Ordering her to kneel by the table, Gilbert took a stool and sat on it. Leaning, with his back to her so she could not see what he was doing, he took up a thin, sharp knife. Jobyna guessed what he would do. It was a common practice to "let" blood. Her father had this done after a fall and a doctor had bled his swollen leg. Sometimes a doctor did this for the sake of purifying the bloodstream. She winced as Gilbert went about his work. The blood spurted into a bowl. Gilbert pressed and massaged her hand.

"Now, that was why it was throbbing and so painful," he told her as he stitched the gash. He bound the hand tightly again. She was shaking uncontrollably from the ordeal. He collected his bag and rinsed the bowl out in the basin, using water from the large pitcher. "You will remember what I have said, won't you, Jobyna?"

Before he opened the door, he said sadly to her, "May your God be with you and help you, Jobyna, Sister of King Luke Chanec."

Gilbert left Jobyna in the room alone. Jobyna wished she could go walking as it would take her mind off the throbbing in her hand which felt worse just now. She gingerly opened the door with her good hand. Her way was instantly barred by two soldiers. "Well, I guess I must stay in here," the captive muttered as she retreated backwards into the room. The door was shut soundly.

Elliad was waiting for Gilbert as the doctor rounded the corner at the end of the corridor to Jobyna's room. He drew Gilbert into a room.

"Well?" he barked. Gilbert nodded sadly.

"Yes," the doctor said, "I told her there was a rescue being planned, and to go with anyone who asked her to accompany them. She trusted me completely, and she told me there are secret passages in the castle. She knows how to access one from the throne room. I feel I would have pushed her too far to ask how to get into the entrance. She may have suspected me."

Elliad was exultant. His plan had worked. He had a philosophy that if one bluff did not work, then try something else. He slapped Gilbert on the shoulder, "You have done very well, man. I am pleased with you. I wish you would take a bag of gold and accept promotion." Gilbert stared at the ground. Elliad felt generous tonight. "Come," he said.

They walked a long distance through the castle and Elliad barked some orders at a K.E. man who was standing guard at a closed door. He turned to Gilbert, handing him a slip of paper. "This is a signed pass for you to leave the castle. You may go to your home; you have earned a rest. Move fast, man, you have 20 minutes to leave!" Elliad turned on his heel and strode off, his personal bodyguards close behind. The K.E. man unlocked the door and Gilbert entered.

"Daddy! Daddy!" He heard the sound of little feet and two children flung themselves into his arms. Tears filled his eyes. Carrying one in each arm, he left the room, anxious to go to his waiting wife, across the castle drawbridge and to his home in the city. He formulated plans to take his young wife and children away from Frencberg to safety.

The man in this castle is a murderous lunatic, he thought. He was sick in his heart. His only consolation was to have been able to do the best he could as a doctor for the girl, and to have told her who John really was. He had been forced to trade the lives of his children for information from Jobyna.

Elliad enjoyed scheming and conniving. His

mind thrived on it.   How easy, he told himself. *"Gentle John" did not work so well, but weak
old Gilbert did, with a little help from his children!
It is a pity Gilbert would not do it without a little
push, but he's really insipid. He won't cause me any
trouble. He's such a weak little man!*

Elliad set his thoughts to the next move he
would make. The vision of King Leopold's
treasure filled his mind with greed and desire.
There had been rumors of such a treasure
chamber but he had never before been sure it
was for real. No matter what happened now,
he wanted those treasures!

He called as many men as could be spared
and they went over the throne room inch by
inch, climbing to every part of the ceiling and
inspecting every engraving on the walls. The
great walls just glared silently at them, unmoving, unyielding.

He left the men there to begin again their
fruitless search for a secret opening. He must
think of a way to get Jobyna to show him how
to get into the secret passages. The plan would
have to be formulated so Jobyna would not
guess she was being set up. First he would see
how his plans to secure the castle were going.
More reports were coming in that Luke Chanec
was gathering a large army, such as had never
been seen in Frencolia. Men from the King's
Castle had deserted their posts and gone to
support the boy. Elliad's men who had been
positioned around the country were coming to

the King's Castle, seeking his protection. Elliad was not so sure he could trust Ruskin any longer as his own men said he was asking suspicious questions and they had seen him talking furtively to men who were supposed to be on duty. When challenged, Ruskin told them he was gaining information for Elliad. Elliad ordered them to have Ruskin and the other knights who had come in with him locked in separate dungeons. He could not risk having anyone around who may cause him trouble. "If they prove to be any hassle in transport to the dungeons," Elliad commanded, "terminate them!"

At heart, Elliad was a great coward. When he had the upper hand, he displayed great power and transmitted fear to those he dominated. He worked well if he was in the majority, especially through tyranny. Now he was facing the fact that the whole country was against him. Since he was personally responsible for the murder of King Leopold, he did not wonder why the bluff labeling the girl was not working. His counter decree was not accepted by Sir Dorai, and a statement had arrived reiterating the demands of the mandate.

Now to the next part of his plan. First he needed some bait. He gathered up some 20 men and together they made a trip from the dungeons to the throne room. Once the task was completed, his actors in place, he went through the maze of corridors to Jobyna's room and burst in. "Jobyna, you're here on your own!" Elliad's voice contained a great element of surprise.

Jobyna had decided she would prepare for bed and had removed her lambskin slippers. "Gilbert was here earlier, but he's gone, . . . John." Jobyna remembered Gilbert's words. Elliad stood at the open door for Jobyna's sake.

"Guards! Guards!" he bellowed. No one came. He went a little way down the corridor and called, "Guards! Guards!" One knight came running along the corridor. Jobyna stood rooted to the spot, wondering what was happening. "Where are the guards I posted outside the girl's door?"

The knight, on cue, replied, "Sire, there is great confusion in the castle. Many of our men are defecting and leaving their posts. Some of them have even taken horses and gone from the castle."

Elliad, seeming to forget Jobyna, rushed off with the knight.

Jobyna peered out into the empty corridor. It was cold and silent. Large wall lamps flickered eerie lights and the distant corner looked uninviting. Jobyna returned for her slippers and cloak. Apprehensively, the girl stepped out into the corridor, following the path Elliad had taken. She half expected him to return with a group of soldiers. How would she find the way to the throne room?

14

Jobyna's heart was in her mouth as she peered down the long stone corridor. Passages like arteries stretched out silently ahead of her. *Which one should I take?* She rounded yet another corner and there in front of her loomed a wide stone staircase. There were no soldiers, no one to hinder her progress. Uncanny emptiness prevailed; her footsteps echoed in the barren halls. Hesitating, an inner voice told her to run back to the room she now knew so well.

Dismissing these thoughts as cowardly, she gingerly descended the stairs. Dim lights cast eerie shadows; her movements looked jerky and stilted. Steadying herself with her uninjured hand, the wall felt cold and unfriendly to her touch. Shaking with fear from the unfamiliar exertion, she reached the foot of the stairs. Jobyna looked around cautiously but even this wing of the castle was void of humanity. The girl did not imagine she was walking into a trap. Not being a deceptive person herself, she found it hard to perceive anyone willfully making harmful plans. Her father had told her often that it was good to give people the benefit of the doubt.

Venturing forward, Jobyna could make out the sound of muffled voices. They seemed to be coming closer, drifting to her from around the next corner. She halted, poised, ready to flee if necessary. The door by her side was slightly ajar and before she had time to resist, a hand reached out its strong bony fingers, digging into her flesh as she was drawn into a room. The two women who had watched her while she was sick were present. This room was similar to the one she had occupied, except there were books on the shelves and it was less clinical in feel and smell.

The sullen woman spoke. It was the first time she had ever spoken directly to Jobyna and used her name. "Jobyna, what are you doing down here? How did you get out of your room?"

"There was no one on guard; there are no soldiers, or anyone, anywhere," Jobyna answered truthfully.

The other woman drew her by the hand, closing the door. "You must hide in here with us."

Jobyna heard footsteps. It sounded as though large numbers of soldiers were coming. The steps were brisk and loud. She could hear the metal of their uniforms and weapons clanking, the heavy sound of their boots marching past the door. The woman opened the door and peering out, said, "They've gone up the stairs. Maybe the king was with them. They will find out you are missing." Turning to Jobyna, she inquired, "Where shall we go?"

Jobyna said, "I don't want to put you at risk, but would one of you show me the way . . . ?"

"Yes, before they come back," the shorter, plump one said cutting her off. "Where?" She eagerly lead Jobyna out into the corridor.

The sullen one stayed in the room. "Not me," she said. Jobyna didn't expect her to volunteer.

The woman who had taken Jobyna's hand was trying hard to be friendly. "My name is Ada. Where can I take you, Jobyna?"

Jobyna realized she did not have many alternatives. She remembered the words Gilbert said to her earlier, *If you are approached by someone, Jobyna, who asks you to go with them, whether it be a soldier, a woman—anyone—then be sure to go.* "To the throne room," she whispered.

Ada looked at her in mock astonishment. "The throne room?" she questioned. (Elliad had told her to show surprise.) "That's not the place for you! It would be too dangerous."

Nevertheless, she led Jobyna along the corridor, away from the stairs.

"Just a moment." Jobyna stopped. Ada looked at her warily. Jobyna whispered, "Where does Elliad keep the Gospel Books, Ada? Do you know?"

This was Ada's moment. "Yes, I do," she replied. "He keeps them in the throne room."

"In the throne room?" Amazement overflowed from Jobyna. Ada thought for a moment Jobyna would guess something was amiss. Things were moving too fast. The girl was not supposed to know the Gospel Books were in the throne room until she arrived there. Ada need not have worried. Jobyna murmured thoughtfully, "Well, I suppose that figures. He probably gloats over them every time he goes there. To him it would be like having a prize prisoner. Take me there, please, Ada."

Ada needed no more prompting. Jobyna was soon breathless. Gasping painfully, she felt a sharp pain in her chest and back. She was lagging behind and as Ada rounded a corner ahead of her, Jobyna stopped, coughing, trying to catch her breath. Ada soon returned and waited until Jobyna was able to carry on. They continued at a slower pace. Every corridor, every stairway they walked on, was deserted. As they traversed along a marble-arched clerestory, Jobyna could see the moon shining. The journey seemed to take forever. Jobyna got a brief idea of the vastness of the King's Castle.

"Just one more stairway and we will be on the level of the throne room," Ada told her, encouraging the exhausted Jobyna. The panting girl was moving slower and Ada would go ahead and wait for her to come. The captive girl was oblivious to the fact that people were monitoring her progress and Elliad already had a gleam of triumph in his eyes. They came to two massive double doors. Even these were unguarded.

Ada pushed one of the doors. It groaned ominously as it swung on its huge hinges. "This is the reception room," she whispered. Jobyna followed her into the chamber. The room was lined with chairs. Walking up the aisle, they came to a massive oblong table blocking the way. Moving around the table, the woman disappeared behind a partition. Jobyna followed apprehensively.

Ada led the way through more doors, down a short, wide hallway and stopped in front of two more double doors like those to the reception room. These doors uttered not a sound as Ada pushed them open. "Here we are."

Jobyna paused and looked around the great Frencolian throne room. Never had she seen such a magnificent place. The splendor and richness of her surroundings froze her to the spot in amazement. Ada grasped her hand, pulling her into the room and closing the doors. This was the formidable place from where Elliad, the demagogue, sounded out his orders and announced his decrees of injustice and murder. Dazzled, the girl walked slowly toward the great throne. It was not an elaborate piece of furniture, but Jobyna realized the tremendous power the one sitting on it held over the lives of the people of Frencolia.

Ada stood back, turning to look at the doors, as Jobyna climbed the marble steps to the throne itself. Instinctively, she knelt and touched the two areas one of the charts had shown. A metal panel slid silently back, revealing a key hole. Realizing what she had done, Jobyna pressed the places again and the panel slipped effortlessly back in place. She was overawed to realize Luke possessed the key to open the step's hidden chamber.

"Jobyna." Ada came closer. She did not want to frighten her, so she waited, speaking quietly, her voice carrying freely in the near-perfect acoustics of the room. "The Gospel Books are just over here."

To the right of a circular dais were large piles of books, all shapes and sizes. Jobyna reverently picked one of them up. She let her fingers linger on the beautiful leather binding. It was a copy of *The Psalms of David*. She reached for another. This was a complete copy of the whole Scriptures. Unbidden tears ran down her cheeks. "Homes all over Frencolia are poor tonight because these great treasures have been removed and brought to this place. Houses have been burned down . . . children left orphans." Ada did not speak; Elliad had told her to let the girl take as long as she needed.

Jobyna dried her eyes, looking around the room. The throne room was well lit, Jobyna supposed the big lamps burned at all times. "How wonderful that there is no one here. We must hide these treasures from Elliad. He must not destroy them." She took for granted that Ada would help her. "Come with me," she commanded.

Jobyna diagonally counted the marble stones from the corner of the room almost to the middle of the floor. She then counted, to herself, seven toward the left wall. Crouching down, she pointed to one of the small octagonal tiles in the corner of a slab. "Ada, place one of your heels here." Pointing to another one at the opposite corner, she continued, "Put the other foot there. Don't move." Jobyna counted diagonally again, three back toward the throne. She then followed the line of slabs out to the wall. The walls of marble slabs had the same octagonal pieces at the corner edges. These were all grooved with "K.F."

Jobyna looked around, feeling the surface of these octagons in comparison to the others. Yes, two were indented more than the rest, the grooves around them very deep. They were about shoulder height for her, waist height for a tall man. Her bandaged hand was unable to grip. Try as she might, nothing moved.

"We'll have to swap places."

Ada walked toward her. Jobyna showed her the two octagons and Ada waited wonderingly as the girl counted out the marble squares once again. "Do whatever she tells you!" Elliad had commanded, and although Ada did not know what was going on, she complied. The woman wished she knew the number and patterns Jobyna had counted out; it was confusing.

Jobyna took her slippers off and placed her heels on the two octagons. She hoped she would be heavy enough to trigger the mechanisms.

"Twist the two together," Jobyna called. "Twist them until the wall opens." Ada twisted the two with all her might and from within the wall, there was a series of clicks. At Ada's side, part of the wall turned inward with a deep rumble, revealing a secret passage.

Jobyna rushed over. "It worked!" Her voice was filled with happy surprise. "Come, we can put all the Gospel Books in there. Ada, please help me."

The books were heavy. Jobyna was tired and still quite weak. Some of them could only be carried one at a time and the job seemed endless. Ada helped her. They stacked them along the wall, making piles of up to 10 with the larger ones on the bottom.

When they were about halfway through the pile, Jobyna came out of the passage to discover she was alone in the throne room. She instantly glanced toward the doors which were swinging closed. Ada had left her.

Jobyna's thoughts raced; she could not decide what to do next. She must hide the Gospel Books and close the secret opening. Should she get more books, or just hide the ones in the passage? Walking toward the remaining Gospel Books, the girl hesitated by the throne. The sound of voices disturbed her indecision. Elliad burst in, followed by several knights. The trembling girl turned and stared, momentarily frozen to the spot. Then she darted for the opening. Fidgeting with the knobs she tried to remember, but Elliad John was there, grabbing her, holding her hands, pinning her arms behind her back, forcing her backwards against the marble wall!

"No!" she cried. "Oh, no!"

15

Elliad was jubilant; everything had gone as he had imagined. Gazing into the dark opening of the secret passage, he grasped Jobyna's hair and pushed her firmly toward Berg.

"Hold her carefully," he cautioned. Turning to the knights, he barked out orders. "Get the torches. I want guards on all doors and double the guard at this entrance." He ran his hand around the marble opening, hesitated a moment, then walked inside. *So this is the secret I should have known as king!* he thought, impatient to continue with his plan.

Ada entered the throne room and showed him as best she could, Jobyna's maneuvers, explaining that it took two to make the slab move. Elliad realized he would not make much progress unless Jobyna told him what to do and where to go. In all probability, a maze of passages lay beneath the castle. He was just as likely to end up in the dungeons with his own prisoners if he was not careful!

"Jobyna, you know the way to King Leopold's treasure, don't you?"

Not waiting for an answer, Elliad commanded, "You will show us how to get there!" Berg tightened his hold on Jobyna and she began coughing helplessly.

The rest of the night was a terrible nightmare for Jobyna. Elliad took six knights with him and the girl was half dragged, half carried, along the dark musty passages, down numerous steps. Most of the men carried torches. The bright flares chased away unwilling shadows that loomed before them. Behaving like a man possessed, Elliad was intent on gaining the prize. He realized there must ultimately be a deep passage, passing under the moat, continuing on for a long distance.

"This must be the one." Elliad pointed his cresset along a dark tunnel. The company turned down the alley. Some of the other passages they had taken ended suddenly at stone walls. In the near darkness, one of the knights tripped and fell. Upon examination, Elliad realized the body of Samuel lay across the path. The body had decomposed and a vile smell filled the passage. Elliad exclaimed they were surely on the right track now. Jobyna retched as she was dragged passed the body. The flesh was almost totally gone from the bones, a green-black mold grew on what tissue was left.

Berg was a huge man. He reminded Jobyna of a mountain. Her feet had to race to keep up with his big strides. The damp earth floor seemed to go on an incline and soon they were climbing. Berg got impatient with her tripping, coughing and sometimes crying. With a grunt he scooped her up in his strong arms and carried her. She wished she could be anywhere else than in the arms of this monster. She tried to pray. *How can God help me?* she thought, brokenly. *Maybe You've forgotten me, Lord.* Unable to think of much else, Jobyna remembered the stream in the valley, flowing, flowing. . . .

When they arrived at yet another dead end, Jobyna had been almost jogged to sleep. It felt to her as though they had been traveling all night. The men examined the wall, pounding on it. Berg dropped Jobyna roughly on the hard clay floor and banged the wall with his huge fists. He kicked the unmoving stones and the other men followed suit.

Elliad eased himself to the ground beside Jobyna. "Jobyna," he said, shaking her shoulders violently, "you must tell us how to get in here!" He needed her help now and he was at a loss. He had tried trickery and torture, what else was there? He would do anything at all to get his heart's desire. "Jobyna, what can I do for you to show me how get into this place?" He stood up, his hand rubbing his chin, his cold blue eyes staring at her.

Jobyna watched the men pressing, thumping and pushing, casting angry glances and curses her way. She realized that they could, by chance, trigger off the opening mechanism, just as she and Luke had in the cave the other side of the chamber. Six men were trying hard and it only took two. If they did open it without her help, then she would certainly be dead. If not, . . . Jobyna did not know which way to turn . . . to tell or not to tell?

"John," she said automatically using the familiar name. Elliad turned around. "How do I know you will do what I want?"

Elliad leaned on the wall, a cynical sneer on his face. He looked down on her. "What is your price?" The men stopped their futile efforts and waited for the wench's response.

"I want you to promise to leave Frencolia and not destroy the Gospel Books."

Elliad hesitated a moment. Then he said, "Is that all you want, Sparrow? How did you know it was I who would destroy the Gospel Books?"

"It is obvious you are Elliad." Jobyna coughed, realizing her slip. "All the men jump to obey your every wish. You fit all descriptions of Elliad." She remembered Luke's likening him to the devil.

Exasperated, Elliad paced along the wall. He said to his men, "I constantly find myself wanting to wring this sorry bird's neck. I have never given in to a woman's whims in my life and I find this creature utterly frustrating! The Gospel Books are useless to me. Frencolia is a lost cause. We have plans that do not include Frencolia, just through that wall."

"One other thing," Jobyna remembered, turning to Elliad's men. "You must not touch the remains of King Leopold."

The men were ready to agree to anything that may grant them passage through this wall. Jobyna knew she could not trust one word any of them said, but if there was a way she could save the Gospel Books, she would sacrifice everything else, including herself. Frencolia could do without the treasures in the cave, but not without the Word of God. She looked around at them all. "I will show you how to get in there if you will give your solemn, truthful word to do these things."

Elliad, hating every word she uttered because he was being told and did not have any other choice but to comply, answered, "Just show us, Jobyna, show us!"

"No," Jobyna retaliated, defying him, "I want to hear you say you will not destroy the Gospel Books, you will leave Frencolia, and you will not harm King Leopold's body."

The six men agreed instantly, "We will . . . we will . . . we won't!"

Elliad, feeling like a defeated knave, knowing she had the upper hand, addressed her seriously, "Jobyna, Daughter of Chanec of Chanoine, if you show us how to get into that treasure cave and the treasures are as marvelous as I believe they are, I, Elliad, will abdicate. I will no longer be king in Frencolia and will go into exile. I will not destroy the Gospel Books and we will not touch the body of Leopold."

His blue eyes were glowing in the orange flame. He folded his arms. A smug look played across his lips. "I am surprised you did not ask for yourself, Sparrow." He turned to his men. "If she shows us what we want to know, she will live." Elliad felt extremely generous tonight.

Jobyna moved to the wall. They held the flares closer as she let her fingers wander over the stones. Elliad watched closely, holding his breath. Suspense silently crept through the earthy atmosphere of the cramped passage. "There is an indent along one of these grooves." Her fingers found the spot. "Here it is." She worked down the vertical grooves. Her eyes met Elliad's. "You place one hand in that groove, and one in this groove; you will feel a small knob." She moved to the corner. There were large pieces of stone missing, as though chipped away, from the bottom row of stones. Jobyna counted along. She turned to Berg, "You put one foot in there . . . and one here. . . . No, someone else. Your feet are too big." Berg had the feet of a giant. One of the others, with a K.E. uniform on, complied. "Now, you must apply the pressure on every point at the same time."

The pressure applied, a grating sound ensued. Half of the great stone wall swung around as though hinged at the top and bottom. If Jobyna had felt stronger she would have made her way back to the throne room for the men ignored her in the wonder of stepping into the treasure cave. Chaos prevailed as lids were pushed open. The clothes Luke and Jobyna had left around the cave were cast aside as gold coin, jewelry and rare treasures were inspected.

Berg heard Jobyna's sigh as she sank to the floor beside the opening, pulling her cloak around her. She saw Berg put his hand on the hilt of his sword and look toward Elliad. Elliad shook his head at him and the moment was past. Elliad dug his hands into a chest filled with unmarked gold coins. He let the bullion trickle through his fingers. The men laughed in delight. Beautiful bracelets, necklaces, broaches, tiaras were "ooohed" and "aaahed" over. Elliad took a jewel-studded cloak and wrapped it around his shoulders.

It was some time before the rapture of their find passed and they finally stopped saying to each other, "Here, look at this!" and "This one is more valuable; look at the diamonds!"

Numb and tired, in shock from all that had happened, Jobyna was exhausted due to the lateness of the hour and her weak physical condition. She wished for a warm bed to curl up in. The men's voices became distant and the sleepy girl jumped with fright as Elliad picked her up in his arms. He sat her on the lid of the chest beside the king's body. Pulling her cloak off, he put a ruby necklace around her neck, struggling impatiently with the catch. Berg sat a diamond tiara on her head. A bulky velvet cloak was placed around her trembling shoulders and Elliad proclaimed in mocking tones, "Let us bow to the Princess Jobyna, who made all of this possible!" They bowed, knelt, laughed and mocked.

Elliad continued, "Look around, Jobyna, these are real treasures! How can a Gospel Book compare? What could such nonsense do for a man that would surpass these treasures?" He did not expect her to answer. The men began carrying the chests through the opening into the tunnel. It was a slow job and hard work even for these fit knights. Elliad decided they would put all the chests through the gap, then go back and get more men to help with the work. He wanted to close the wall as soon as possible so others did not know about the cave or see the king's body.

Jobyna sat on the floor and pulled the cloak around her. In spite of the work going on in the cave, she was soon fast asleep.

The sun rose many hours before Elliad had the last chest carried into the heavily guarded

168

throne room. He was so happy, he was almost beside himself with ecstasy. The power, the glory, the trust that he placed in these treasures! He could have anything he wanted! Never before had food been consumed in the throne room, but Elliad sent for food and drink and they celebrated until noon.

Jobyna woke up unrefreshed but warm as toast. Wondering for a split second where she was, she felt mortified as she recalled the events of the night. The dark cave was now empty but for the king's body. Groping her way along, she stumbled on garments strewn here and there. She found the wall which opened out into the cave in the valley. Feeling blindly for the two knobs, the girl tried to make the opening mechanism work. Her efforts were unrewarded, nothing budged. Her tortured hand was too weak and stiff. Fumbling her way around the huge cave, Jobyna almost fell over the body.

The other exit was the same. The stone mass was unyielding and still. With no flint to light any of the lamps, the darkness engulfed her, pressing heavily on her slight frame. Sinking back to the floor, pulling the tiara from her head, Jobyna realized her predicament.

What a liar, she thought, crying to herself. She wished Berg had used his sword and killed her there and then. Now she was left here, to die slowly. Her misery increased greatly as she thought about the Gospel Books. *Elliad was such a deceiver*, she thought, *he will burn the books just to spite me.* The negative thoughts whirring in her mind brought crushing depression. Her mouth was dry and she longed for the cool water of the stream in the valley. It had been a long time since she had eaten anything and the grumbling of her stomach reminded her of this fact.

This place was going to see the death of a second person. In extreme desolation, she realized no one else knew how to enter the cave. Even if Luke came to the valley, he did not know how the cave opened. Knowing Luke as she did, she hoped he would figure it out. But she remembered he was far away right now. This place was surely to be her tomb. She imagined herself slowly dying, wasting away, dehydration taking its toll. In her mind she could already feel the pain ravaging her body and death setting in. Each breath she took felt as though it did not register in her lungs. She began to gulp the stale air, a breathless sensation gripping her. She slumped to the ground, sleep—just sleep—she willed herself.

16

Elliad congratulated himself over and over while he sat on the throne. His mind was working ahead to where he would go and what he would do. He had spoken truly to Jobyna. To him Frencolia was a lost cause. These riches would buy him great power and renown but he knew it would not be here, in the kingdom of Frencolia. Aware of barely four days more for him to act without his life being at extreme risk, he began making hasty plans with his men. Much later in the day, he remembered Jobyna. She did not have any value, or use to him, . . . or did she?

Jobyna remembered her mother telling her that when she was depressed and could do nothing to change the circumstances, she should make her mind think of something, anything, that she could be thankful about. Thankfulness, she was told, would banish the clouds of depression. Jobyna was disillusioned with life. What could she be thankful for in a place like this? If only she could get her mind off this cave with its dead body and haunting memories. *Luke!* She would think of Luke. How thankful she was to know that he was safe. Then she thought of God. Maybe she was just a little sparrow, but God had said in His Word that He knew all about the sparrows and not one of them was away from His caring eye. *Yes, God cared! Wasn't Joseph thrown into a pit by his very own brothers?* Jobyna was sure she felt as Joseph must have before one of his brothers hauled him out of the pit. Remembering that this same brother sold Joseph into slavery, the girl decided she would think about something else. What wonderful memories she had of her family life . . . especially when her two brothers and sister had been alive . . . before the disease that swept through the country.

The time slowly passed, and Jobyna began singing softly. She reaffirmed her philosophy regarding her life. "If I die—I live! There is nothing to lose!" she whispered into the darkness.

Suddenly, the great wall swung open! Followed by his knights carrying torches, Elliad entered the tomb. Before Jobyna could move, he dragged the frightened girl to her feet. Elliad pushed a flask toward her and she drank thirstily, letting the cool water trickle down her parched throat. While she savored the liquid, the men walked to the wall by the exit.

Elliad spoke to her, "We cannot find the maps and charts of the kingdom among the treasures!" He grasped her shoulders and shook her violently. "Where are they? Where did you put the Gospel Book with the documents of the kingdom?" Shaking her harder, he bellowed, "Are they out in the valley?"

The thought of this man gaining possession of such valuable information caused Jobyna to shake her head. A feeling of faintness flooded her frame. Her body grew limp under her oppressor's vice-like grip and as he released his hold, the girl fell helplessly to the floor. He believed she may have taken the book away from the valley. By now someone else may have possession of the maps! Elliad worried now that others may find their way to the cave and eventually to the throne room! He would have to move fast to keep control over all his treasures!

Glittering diamonds caught his eye! He snatched the tiara up and strode to Berg, who had the girl cradled in his massive arms, waiting to move off. Pushing the headpiece once again on his princess's head, Elliad's scornful voice came to the girl, as though from a universe of darkness. "I came back for the last treasure, Sparrow. You are valuable to me!" He motioned for his men to gather remaining garments off the floor.

Jobyna could hardly believe her eyes when they emerged from the dark tunnel. The throne room was in chaos! Servants and slaves were sorting through the treasure chests, and valuables were being packed into smaller, light cases and bags. Receptacles were in the process of being bound and secured with leather bindings. One could scarcely hear oneself think in the commotion! The room had the appearance of a peasant's market place. Plates and goblets lay smashed on the marble tiles! Scraps and leftovers from what looked to have been a sumptuous meal were strewn everywhere. Puddles of wine darkened the floor, and Jobyna, still feeling dizzy and shaky, feared she may slip on the sticky substance. The room reeked of alcohol and body odor. On one of the beautiful wall tapestries, Jobyna's eyes focused on the splattered presence of some sort of stew.

"Eat something, Sparrow!" Elliad bellowed, indicating the dried-out leftovers on one of the many plates.

The men and women looked up from their work. They observed a thin, gaunt, trembling slip of a girl, wearing a sparkling diamond tiara on her dishevelled hair. An outsized deep crimson velvet cloak trailed along the marble floor behind her.

Jobyna glanced around the throne room. Above her head, set into the ceiling was a magnificent dome of stained glass, allowing the retiring sun to seep colorfully down and play rainbows on the marble walls. Her eyes went to the throne. Instinctively, she took a step toward the remaining Gospel Books. She turned to see what Elliad was doing. He was watching her, his eyes not missing a thing. Lowering her head, she walked toward the food, feeling she must not draw his attention to the Gospel Books lest he destroy them in a fit of rage. Hungrily eating some chicken pieces and bread, she was thankful that Elliad was letting her eat at all.

To die slowly in the cave had been Jobyna's expectation, and this sudden change in circumstances made her feel strangely off balance. The servants returned to their work and the girl noticed as they went in and out, soldiers accompanied them. There were at least two soldiers for every person in the place, she calculated.

The food and drink gave her vitality and strength; what would she do next? The Gospel Books were on her mind constantly and she found herself moving closer to them every time Elliad glanced the other way. He was studying some of the coins with a group of men who were referring to books containing drawings of coinage. She supposed the coins were from other countries, or maybe they were very old. Her hand reached out and tenderly touched the cover of one of the Gospel Books. She picked it up and sat on the bottom step. *Nothing could replace these treasures*, Jobyna thought. Opening the book, she read the words of wisdom in beautiful script on the pages. How much she loved the words from the *Book of the Proverbs*. With wide eyes, she read from the 10th chapter: "Treasures of wickedness profit nothing: but righteousness delivereth from death." Thumbing a little way back, she felt comforted as she read words from the *Book of the Psalms*.

Elliad saw Jobyna, asleep on the bottom step of the great dais, her head resting forward on the pages of the open book she nestled in her lap. The Gospel Books no longer worried him. The joy of his captured treasures filled his thoughts and possessed his mind. He felt sure he had done the right thing in going back to the cave for Jobyna, the trump treasure. She was his ticket to safety and future trade with anyone trying to cause him trouble. He had changed his mind about the sparrow. The sister of the new king of Frencolia was a worthwhile treasure to take care of!

17

Jobyna was escorted to an apartment at the back of the castle that night. A set of three rooms revealed a dining/sitting room, a bedroom and a bathroom, brightly painted and lavishly furnished. A small round marble bath-tub was set into the floor of the bathroom. Servants were filling it with hot water. Herbs and flowers were sprinkled in as the water was poured from large pottery urns.

As in a trance, Jobyna soaked her tired limbs in the fragrant, tepid waters. The aroma soothed her aching body and overwrought mind. She tried to remember how long it had been since she had indulged in the simple pleasure of a bath. The manor house had one bath only, a huge wooden tub with handles on it so it could be carried around from room to room. Servants spent hours heating enough water for the bath. For the economy of the whole exercise, several people would use the same water. Jobyna had never seen a bath like this one before. She had seen drawings of baths like it in a book about ancient Roman times.

Jobyna lay back, letting the water wash away her worries. She reminded herself to be like the stream and right now, to accept where the current was running was wonderful. A slave girl wearing a round gold earring bearing the initials K.E., dried Jobyna's hair and patted it with a large soft, velvety towel. Jobyna would have done it herself, but the slave girl firmly held on to the towel until Jobyna released it.

Rubbing oil into Jobyna's back, the slave then combed her hair until it shone in the candle light. The girl also carefully rebound Jobyna's hand with a fresh cloth bandage. Jobyna studied the slave girl while she tended to her needs. It puzzled her that the maid did not speak.

The beautiful silk nightgown, satin sheets, feathered mattress and satin-covered pillows contrasted greatly to the night Jobyna had spent in the cave sleeping on the cold, hard floor. Even compared to the small, gray-walled room she had been in while she was sick, this was so very fabulous, beyond her wildest imaginations. She dare not allow her thoughts to wonder as to the reason of all this luxury for her, a prisoner. It was so good, so unexpected. She remembered that she must thank God for the good things, too! Nothing could be taken for granted. The silent slave girl curled up on a mat beside her bed. As Jobyna heard the scrupulous soldiers change guard outside the door she slowly sank into slumber surrounded by the softness of satin sheets.

Except for long escorted walks, twice daily, along the corridors of the castle, Jobyna was confined to her room. A tempting variety of food was offered her and she ate until satisfied. The rose color returned to her cheeks and she felt totally rested. The crimson cloak had been taken away. It was returned having been altered to fit properly. A woman calling herself "Boey" bustled in and measured Jobyna, chatting cheerfully all the time. Jobyna asked what all the measurements were for?

"Oh, I'm not allowed to answer any questions, luv. Just you relax, everything is going to be all right," Boey answered.

This obscure answer mystified Jobyna. Boey continued to bustle in and out, bringing dresses of all colors and styles for Jobyna to try on. It was obvious the clothes had been altered for her. *What was going on? What was going to happen?* Jobyna remembered she must go wherever the current took her; the answer would be just around the corner.

The slave girl's big brown eyes never left Jobyna. She was constantly there to do everything she could for her mistress, not allowing Jobyna to comb her hair, or pull on slippers herself. Jobyna could not bear the silence between her and the girl. When they were alone in the room she entreated, "Please tell me your name . . . please." The girl shook her head, her black curls covering her eyes. "Please talk to me, I need someone to talk to!"

The girl's wide eyes stared into Jobyna's as she continued, "You have no idea what I've been through. I just need someone to talk to." The girl took Jobyna's hand and led her to the couch. Once Jobyna was seated, the slave knelt in front of her and opened her mouth.

The slave pointed inside, making a guttural, gurgling noise, "Uh, ug." Instinctively Jobyna closed her eyes, her stomach churning.

Jobyna grasped the girl's hand in hers. "I want to be your friend."

The slave girl backed off shaking her head as Jobyna continued talking. "I am a prisoner, too. There is no difference between you and me." Then Jobyna remembered. "Did Elliad have that done to you?" The girl hung her head, the black curls obscuring her vision. "Well, he did this to me." Jobyna held up her bandaged hand. "He would have broken all my fingers. He said he'd have my tongue. He may just do it, too, I suppose." Tears flowed down the slave girl's cheeks. She knelt on the floor by Jobyna's feet, her fingers gently stroking Jobyna's arm above the bandage.

Boey rushed in, disturbing the two. The slave girl sprang to her feet, a guilty look on her face.

"What is this girl's name?" Jobyna asked Boey.

"Nobody knows, she can't tell." Boey answered, carelessly. "Who cares anyway; she's just a slave."

To Boey's surprise, Jobyna said obstinately, "Well, I care. A person needs a name."

"A slave isn't a person. A slave is a thing, like a horse, or some furniture," Boey responded sharply. "And it's not fitting for one of your station to be speaking like this."

Jobyna did not understand the servant's thinking, but she felt severely reprimanded. Boey was about the age her mother would have been, and Jobyna knew she was being treated like a child. Her father had servants who were on the manor payroll or worked for their board and keep. She knew of other barons who owned slaves, but her father had declared his slaves "free-men" when he became a believer.

When Boey finally left the room, Jobyna said to the girl, "I am going to call you 'Ellice,' which means 'Jehovah is God.' Is that all right

181

with you?" The girl nodded in submission. Jobyna continued, "You do need a name. I just can't say, 'Hey you with the brown eyes' can I?" The girl smiled a sad smile, her lips pressed tightly closed.

Jobyna chatted on to Ellice, telling her about her parents and home. "My Mother's name was Elissa, which means 'Consecrated to God.' Elliad had my parents killed because they would not give him our Gospel Books."

"How old are you? Just nod when I get to your age," Jobyna questioned. She began at 15, but the girl shook her head until Jobyna came to 21. "You look much younger." Her age amazed Jobyna. Not yet 14, Jobyna was much taller. After all the newly named Ellice had gone through, maybe she had not grown very tall, Jobyna mused.

She avoided talking about Luke, but she thought of him often and prayed for his well-being. "Most of all," she prayed, "May he feel You are with him, Lord."

The safety of his sister was a constant worry to Luke. There were two days left before Sir Dorai and all the armies of Frencolia would march to Frencberg and declare open war against Elliad. No word came from Ruskin or anyone else in the King's Castle. The message arrived through Sir Dorai that the King's Castle was in a state of siege. No messages had been sent into the castle and none had come out since the counter-decree. If Luke's sister was going to be executed at the end of the week, there were just 48 hours remaining.

Luke dispatched a message to Sir Dorai, asking if he could join him at the Knight's Tower. If Elliad had secured the castle in siege, then surely there would be no threat to anyone traveling. The country had united against the tyrant; it must be reasonably safe for Luke to journey closer.

Sir Dorai's reply to Luke's request was a simple "no." He emphasized that the roads were not safe and that some of the people were undecided about their loyalties and there were skirmishes among the soldiers. Frequent reports were coming in—theft, homes being ransacked, assaults and murders. Sir Dorai reinforced in his letter to Luke that this crime wave was due to the unrest and uncertainty which prevailed. He would send for Luke or come himself the instant it was safe.

Jobyna returned to her quarters, feeling rejuvenated and energetic, after a long walk.

Ellice had walked with her and two soldiers followed a small margin behind. Out on the battlements, the fresh air was invigorating and Jobyna was refreshed. The view from the back of the King's Castle looked over lush green farmland. Jobyna saw trees bursting with beautiful blossoms and the signature of fresh new life was splashed across the landscape. It rested her mind just looking at the green countryside.

A messenger came out and ordered Jobyna to return to her rooms. The servants were preparing the bath and she was to dress for dinner with the king. The meal was being served early and she must not be late. Jobyna did not dare do anything else but comply. She walked briskly back to the apartment. She noticed the doors now open along the corridor, revealing a number of suites near hers, also sporting views out on to the Frencolian farmland.

Ellice helped Jobyna dress. Boey waited to view the completed work. The gown was of cream wool lace, loose fitting, with satin petticoats. Ellice placed the ruby necklace gently around her neck. Boey gave the slave girl a red rose to fix in Jobyna's hair at the back of the diamond tiara.

Boey said, "You'll do. You just need a little more meat on your bones. But then, you'll fill out as you get older."

Jobyna was filled with apprehension as she made the long walk, escorted of course, to the castle's dining room. Upon arrival at the reception room to the great hall, a knave took the crimson cloak from her slender shoulders and ushered her into the room. The magnificence of the dining room overawed Jobyna, causing her to halt in her steps.

Enormous crystal chandeliers with hundreds of brilliantly lit candles hung from the brightly decorated ceiling. The light danced and flickered on the walls.

She was summoned back to the present as a voice resounded, "Jobyna, Captive Princess of King Elliad!"

Everyone—that is, except Elliad—stood to their feet. The knave, a young lad about Jobyna's age, extended his arm and Jobyna placed her hand on his, palm down, the custom Jobyna had been taught for special occasions. He escorted her around to the huge table at the front of the hall to the seat beside Elliad. Jobyna's heart was in her mouth. She had to work hard to make herself walk toward him. With her head held high, she met his icy blue eyes. He stood, bowing to her, took her hand and giving it a mock kiss, motioned for her to sit beside him. Once she was seated, Elliad sat down. Everyone else in the dining room sat.

The hot food was brought in and people began eating. Jobyna's emotions were too stirred up for her to feel hungry. She began to inspect the company. Almost all those at the dinner were men, just a few women here and there. Not far from where she sat, she recognized Ada, and the other woman, the sullen one. Berg was there, and she looked for Ruskin, her eyes searching every face.

Elliad's deep voice pulled her back to her table, "The sparrow must eat if the sparrow would be strong." Jobyna cast her attention to the food before her and made up her mind to enjoy herself and make the most of time out of her quarters.

"How does the sparrow find her nest?" Elliad asked.

Quickly swallowing her mouthful, Jobyna answered, "Very good thank you. It has been much better. I mean . . . I am . . . the apartment is lovely."

"You will need to go to sleep early tonight," Elliad said softly. "Tomorrow before daybreak, I am leaving Frencolia. You are coming with me, Jobyna." Elliad paused while Jobyna tried hard not to choke on the dessert she was partway through swallowing. He raised his forefinger as a warning for her to keep silent. Her green eyes were full of fear and questions.

"You will do exactly as you are told, Jobyna. If anyone asks you your name, you are to tell them you are 'The Princess Jobyna, Sister of King Luke Chanec of Frencolia.' You see, Jobyna, you are my passport to safety." Jobyna opened her mouth to interject but he shook his head, "There will be no questions at all. You obey! Do you understand?" Elliad's menacing tone silenced Jobyna. Questions circled through her mind. She did not feel anger, but tried to think what emotion it was that she felt. Maybe she couldn't feel anything anymore.

She remembered, *God is in control*. Maybe help would come before morning. If not, she would have to go with Elliad, moving further away from Luke and freedom.

Elliad's voice came to her again, "Jobyna, I asked you a question!"

"Oh, I'm sorry, my mind wandered," Jobyna apologized.

"I asked if you understood! You are to answer when asked a question!"

"Yes, I do understand, and I will try to remember." Jobyna spoke with a humble voice but her top lip curled and disdain shadowed her face. She hung her head. It was not worth making Elliad angry at her. That would achieve nothing but to make her life more miserable.

Jobyna returned to her apartment to find several large trunks just inside the door. Looking around, she saw that furnishings, curtains, tapestries, rugs and other items had been folded or rolled up and tied in small bundles.

Boey was talking to Ellice, "I'll be in soon after midnight and we will put the sheets and pillowcases in the trunk." She turned to Jobyna. "Make sure you get to sleep as soon as possible. You'll need all the rest you can get."

As soon as Boey left, Jobyna turned to Ellice. "I need to write my brother, Luke, a note. Do you know where I can get some paper, a quill and ink?" Ellice screwed her face up, obviously trying to make up her mind. If she was caught out of Jobyna's apartment, she would be severely punished and her new mistress would be in trouble.

Remembering Boey's frantic packing, she went to the trunks and opened one. Feeling around in the clothing, finding nothing, she closed the lid. The next trunk was full of things Boey had collected from other apartments. Several quills had been placed on top and there were bottles of ink wrapped in the rugs. In another trunk, sheaves of paper, rolled tightly and tied with ribbon, had been placed to take up spare spaces.

Jobyna imagined the whole castle had been ransacked and nothing of value would be left. She chose a piece of fine parchment, drew the lamp close to her, and compiled a letter to Luke.

How much love could one give in a letter? How could she convey that she wanted more than anything to stay in Frencolia with him? She must tell him she would pray for him every day, and that she believed they would meet again. She must inform him of the Gospel Book in the valley and instruct him where to find it. What if someone else found her letter? Luke and Frencolia needed the charts. Completing the words for the last of her family on earth, she left a large space then wrote in her flowery handwriting,

> My heart is full of the treasures of God's Word. I am hidden in the cleft of the Rock. Though I walk through the valley of the shadow of death, I will fear no evil. God is the one who charts and maps our lives.

She made appropriate underlinings and hoped Luke would understand.

> Signed in deep love,
> your affectionate little sister,
> Jobyna.

Jobyna rolled the parchment and fastened it with ribbon.

"Ellice, where can we hide it so no one will find it?" They examined the room. Moving to the bedroom, Ellice pointed to the doorway. Above the opening was a transom, which Jobyna had not noticed before.

Together they dragged the table to the doorway and placed a square stool on the smooth top. Jobyna carefully placed the roll on the ledge of the transom, out of sight. She sighed as they pushed the table and chair back to their respective places. How could she direct Luke to look there? He may never know she had even been in this room. Utter helplessness flooded the captive for a moment. Then she remembered the kingdom charts; how dots and letters were used to guide. Writing with the quill once more, Jobyna wrote a large black "J" on the top of the wooden table. She would have drawn an arrow on the inside of the bedroom door, pointing to the transom, but knew that would be too obvious, so she drew a "J" upside down.

Feeling she had done her best, she turned to her bed. Ellice packed the things back into the trunks and they prepared for sleep. Kneeling to pray, Jobyna realized this may be her last night in Frencolia. The story of Joseph came to mind once more as she lay down to sleep. He too, was stolen away from his country. God did not forsake Joseph, but used the bad deed for His good! *God is in control,* she thought.

Awakened by an urgent voice, Jobyna heard Boey demanding the sheets which she wanted to pack in the last of the trunks. Jobyna found it hard to rouse herself. She desperately wanted to sleep. Ellice helped her dress, having laid aside a plain brown woolen dress and loose fitting jacket. Jobyna recognized the boots as her own, the ones she had worn to the King's Castle. Ellice wore a simple wool dress and riding boots. She carried her own plain brown cloak and Jobyna's crimson one. Servants came and carried the trunks away.

The next few hours seemed a confused dream to Jobyna. Boey stayed with them and cautioned Jobyna to keep completely silent. The slave girl placed Jobyna's cloak around her shoulders and motioned for her to pull the hood over her copper brown hair.

The courtyard at the back of the King's Castle was a seething mass of people, horses and carts. Torches burning here and there were fastened to the walls, casting limited light on the industrious people. Horse-drawn carts were moving off across the moat bridge. The only sound permeating the cool night air was the clatter of the horses' hooves, the snorting and whinnying, and the sound of the cartwheels as they moved off. No one spoke. Trunks, bags, and packs were loaded and tied down. The whole exodus was progressing like clockwork, smoothly, quickly. Jobyna saw Elliad riding toward her, leading a horse beside him.

"Brownlea," Jobyna whispered as the horse came near. The horse nuzzled her in a familiar way. Vapor from the animal's nostrils rose in the frosty air. Stroking his nose gently, Jobyna felt she had found a long lost friend.

Elliad pointed to Ellice. "You'll ride this one, slave." Then to Boey, "Get on the cart woman. Don't dawdle."

He dismounted, and Jobyna recognized his horse. "Speed! This is Luke's horse!"

Elliad lifted her on to Speed's back. "Yes, your father had a good herd of horses." He mounted behind her. Jobyna was overwhelmed by a terrible sinking feeling. Elliad was making sure there was no chance of her escaping. He turned Speed, who trotted off over the moat bridge, his hooves echoing out a hollow song.

The back exit of the castle opened on to the city orchards, gardens and farmland. Within minutes they were clear of Frencberg. The road they took grew narrow quickly and there was only just room for the carts to traverse some places. Elliad rode near the back of the company. Jobyna guessed the mounted soldiers she had seen in the courtyard would be traveling behind them. Jobyna had no idea how many people were involved, but she realized there was an atmosphere of finality. This was the end. Elliad really was leaving Frencolia. Tears rolled down her cheeks as she held on to Speed's mane with her right hand. *It would be good for Frencolia,* she thought, *and for Luke, to be rid of Elliad.*

The stretching sun was sending out golden shafts of morning light when Elliad reigned Speed to an halt. He turned the horse around on a rocky platform beside the path, allowing others to pass. A triumphant smile covered his face and his eyes shone with victory. He had done it! Soldiers he left to guard the King's Castle would just now be conveying his communication to the Frencolian knights. If the knights believed this message, he would have another week, at least, before anyone came in pursuit. The soldiers remaining behind had been promised great reward if they followed through with Elliad's orders. They would leave Frencberg in just under one week to join him, leaving two days before the next deadline.

In the expanding morning light, Jobyna could see they had climbed some way and were able to view a breathtaking panorama of the kingdom of Frencolia. The King's Castle was far away in the distance, a small gray pebble surrounded by lush green. To the north, the sleepy smoke from the fireplaces of Ahren—the "eagle" city on a hill—rose lazily in spirals, hovering peacefully above the horizon. North of Ahren was a Knight's Tower.

Elliad did not speak, but Jobyna's heart cried out, *Goodbye Frencolia. Goodbye Luke!* She knew they were at the eastern border and within a few short minutes, Frencolia would be a memory. Elliad had chosen the shortest route to the closest unguarded border. The moment of silent farewell was over. As Elliad urged the horse on into another country, the tears flowed unheeded down Jobyna's cheeks. It was a tearful traverse for the captive princess.

18

Just 24 hours before the deadline! This sobering thought forced Luke to wake from his slumbering. The short span of time and the imminent events forced Luke's mind to remain active. Tension was growing each minute and Sabin tried hard to remind his charge to "Cast all your care on the Lord God."

Shortly before midday, Sir Dorai received a message from the King's Castle. Just after dawn, the message had been lowered by a rope from the tower at the main entrance to the castle. The message read, "I, Elliad John Pruwitt, with the advice of my counselors, have decided for the sake of the kingdom of Frencolia, to gc into exile."

Sir Dorai looked up from the paper. "Elliad has decided to go into exile!" he exclaimed to the other senior knights, Frencolian knights and soldiers there with him. The courtyard at the Knight's Tower at Mayhew erupted into a cheering mass. Sir Dorai returned to the reading of the paper. As he read, a frown darkened his countenance.

Due to the suddenness of your request for my exile I ask for an extension of one week. There are preparations to be made and I cannot complete them all in the short time I have left, namely one day. In return for this week's extension, I promise Jobyna Chanec's life shall be spared. I also ask there be no troops in Frencberg and the exits from the King's Castle be free from obstruction of any kind. I plan to leave Frencolia in six days' time and request no interference.

Signed, Elliad John Pruwitt, Exiled King.

Sir Dorai said, "To answer this request, we need an urgent meeting of the senior knights and lords. For the time being, all troops are to be kept at bay. Those in the city must be unobtrusive, but watchful." Sir Dorai felt Elliad was pushing his luck as far as he could with such a request, but it was a great victory for Frencolia that the man had conceded defeat without fighting. He decided to place reinforcement troops closer to the city, blocking off all roads out of the capital with strict orders to hold anyone coming out of the King's Castle itself, until the leaders decided whether or not to agree with Elliad's terms.

The meeting that night was short, the decision quickly made. All were unanimous. For the sake of peace, they agreed to Elliad's terms. Lord Farey put it very well, "If we do not accept his terms, we go to war. The girl, Jobyna, will surely be killed, wives and mothers all over Frencolia bereaved. Even when our troops win the King's Castle after the siege, the country will be the poorer for it. One week is not long to wait and see if Elliad will keep his word or not. We will be all the more prepared. The positives far outweigh the negatives."

Sir Dorai compiled a statement addressed to Elliad, stating his terms were acceptable. However, he would be escorted to the border by Frencolian troops only after the girl, Jobyna Chanec, was released. The statement was countersigned by all senior knights and the five lords. Sir Dorai knew Elliad would accept their word. The statement was immediately dispatched to the King's Castle.

Later in the day, Sir Dorai received word that the pouch had been drawn up by soldiers at the castle. At this stage, Sir Dorai had no idea Elliad was already out of Frencolia, having taken Luke's sister with him.

Luke received the news of the week's extension the following morning. He felt incredible relief. Jobyna must still be alive; there was hope after all. He was happy there would be no bloodshed. Sir Dorai also wrote that he would send a company of soldiers to bring Luke back to his castle at Leroy and later in the week, to the castle in Samdene. He wanted Luke closer at hand so that when Elliad left, there would be no doubts among the people as to who was now king. Luke was glad to think something was happening. He was getting closer, he thought, to a reunion with his sister.

The next day, Luke rode into the streets of Leroy. The streets were lined with soldiers holding back cheering masses of men, women and children of all ages. They threw blossom petals in his path and great happiness showed on their faces. News of Elliad's exile and of the boy-king's ascension to the throne of Frencolia had been broadcast far and wide. The reign of terror was coming to an end.

A voice from the crowd called, "God bless King Luke Chanec!" In the hysteria of the moment, the crowds echoed the cry. Their cheers grew louder and louder, increasing in urgency.

Luke drew his horse to a halt, the animal's hooves crushing the delicate blossoms. He pivoted in the saddle and looked back over hundreds of unfamiliar faces. "God bless Frencolia!" the boy cried, his arm raised above his head.

Luke was shown to an elaborate guest's apartment in Sir Dorai's castle. Security at the castle was intense; armed guards seemed to be around every corner. Preparations had been made for Luke's arrival. Sir Keith greeted Luke with great warmth. He introduced him to two knights in Sir Dorai's office who were to be Luke's personal bodyguards. However, the boy told Sir Keith he wished Sabin to stay close to him.

Sir Keith brought Luke up to date with other details of events in the kingdom. Luke also indulged in the luxury of a bath in a wooden tub, reminding him of home in the manor house.

The week dragged on painfully, the anticipation relieved somewhat by the uneventful journey to Samdene. The countryside was fragrant with the vapors of spring. Newborn lambs frolicked in the fields, suckling their mothers. Luke loved the Frencolian countryside and the journey made him feel refreshed, his spirits uplifted.

The day before Elliad was supposed to leave, Sir Dorai decided to travel to Frencberg himself. He chose a road out of view from the castle battlements. Headquarters had been set up by Sir Dorai's men, about half a mile from the main gates of the castle. A wool trader in the city had made his empty warehouse available for them.

One of Sir Dorai's knights told his superior that a small company of soldiers had left the castle from the eastern exit just after midnight. "Some 50 or so, but the men were not sure. They did not want to pursue unless you gave the word. There were no carts, just soldiers on horseback," the knight informed Sir Dorai.

Well aware that Elliad could be working some trickery, Sir Dorai nevertheless decided to wait the agreed time. He would use the time of waiting to make inquiries. "I need a man who knows the city inside out," Sir Dorai told the wool trader, named Iven. Iven left the warehouse and returned with an old man he introduced as Lazare.

From his pouch, Sir Dorai removed the chart they had found in the valley and laid it before Lazare. The old man poured over the drawing, his finger tracing every line. He turned it this way and that, holding it close to the lamp.

"Ha. Yes," he said and directed his finger along a dotted line. "This is the castle moat, I feel. And this is some sort of path to the King's Castle. It comes from an opening along here, maybe on the river bank. There are houses along there. I cannot be sure which one it would be. Maybe this." He pointed to an "M" drawn on the dotted line. "Yes, this may be the moat bridge. That means this sort of dotted 'W' here is on the northern side of the moat bridge. The starting point for this path must come from a house across the road from the moat."

Sir Dorai folded the paper, his brow furrowed with thought. It would be too obvious, and maybe premature, for him to search the houses in that area just yet. He would wait for the morrow. Elliad was to leave the castle in the morning.

All four moat bridges to the castle remained closed throughout the night. The reports Sir Dorai received from his men, posted in watch, were encouraging. Nothing was amiss or astir. The morning faded into noon; still there was nothing. Sir Dorai rode around the King's Castle moat, checking with his men. Each report corroborated with the previous; there were no soldiers in the towers, none on the gates, and none on the battlements. The King's Castle looked deserted. Sir Dorai imagined they were getting ready to leave, but his intuition told him to be ready for trickery. Maybe there were other secret exits from the castle. His mind went to the chart.

Returning to the main gate, he ordered his men to search the houses along the road. They were to enter all the rooms and gardens and look for any sign of trap doors or anything unusual.

Early on in the search, he was directed to a house some way from the main gate, inhabited by a widow, her son and his wife, and three grandchildren. In the tiny backyard the soldiers had spied a dry well. Sir Dorai instantly realized the significance of this, so close to the moat river. There was a steel ladder down the inside wall of the well and his soldiers informed him the well was very deep. It was empty, the bottom bone dry. This was the answer to the dotted "W," he thought. He had his men fetch a torch and descended the ladder himself. The bottom of the shaft was square, lined with great slabs of stone. Ascending the ladder, Sir Dorai decided to question the occupants of the house.

"Morna, my mother-in-law, has been sick for almost two years. She does not get out of her bed now. Her mind is almost gone and our doctor says she will not be with us much longer." The woman told Sir Dorai they had lived in the house since she married the son, Gibson, some 10 years ago. She had been 12 years old then. Gibson's father had been a soldier for King Leopold but had been killed in an accidental fall from his mount, just after Elliad proclaimed himself king.

Sir Dorai instantly had his own thoughts and suspicions as to how the soldier had died, but he kept his peace and listened to Rose. Her husband, a tentmaker by trade, was away working. The firm had been very busy making new tents as King Elliad had bought them completely out of both their used and new tents. This information was very significant to Sir Dorai. He asked if he may speak to the widow-mother, Morna.

"I don't think you'll get very much from her, she just raves on so," the woman muttered.

"Just one more question, Rose," Sir Dorai asked. "How often did King Leopold come to the house here?" The daughter-in-law's instant reaction surprised him.

"How do you know about that?" Rose snapped.

"We are still searching for King Leopold's body and we think there may be some sort of passage from your house to the castle. The king did come here, didn't he?"

"Yes. It was mainly at night, very rarely in the day. Mother said we must never tell anyone." She hung her head. "Before her mind wandered, Mother said that King Elliad had threatened her not to tell anyone.'

"How close was your father to the king?" Sir Dorai asked.

"Father was one of King Leopold's bodyguards."

Sir Dorai was satisfied this was all he needed to know. Rose led him down a narrow hall to a small bedroom at the side of the house. "Mother, Morna." She shook the tiny frame on the bed gently. "A man is here to talk to you."

"Leave us," Sir Dorai commanded Rose. He gestured for the soldier at the door to shut it. The room was sparsely furnished and he pulled the lone chair closer to the bed.

"Morna, I am Sir Dorai, a friend of King Leopold." The woman's glazed eyes stared at him in a weird, unseeing way.

"Gilroy, Gilroy, why did you make me do it?"

"What did I make you do, Morna?"

"Gilroy, are you . . . Gilroy?"

"Yes, Morna, tell me about it," Sir Dorai lied, and thus the sordid story unraveled. It was as Sir Dorai expected, but he had not thought it would be revealed so soon. King Leopold and Samuel would come to the house through the tunnel at the back and Gilroy would accompany them on various missions. Gilroy never entered the well, but yes, Samuel of Samdene was always with the king.

"Elliad is really to blame, isn't he, Morna?" Sir Dorai asked.

"Yes, Gilroy, but you know that, don't you?"

"Elliad gave you the poison, didn't he, and you put it in their drink when Samuel and the king came to the house?" It all seemed too simple. Sir Dorai resolved he must have this information properly documented.

The woman rolled on her side, turning her face to the wall. She mumbled her guilt and cried, "He was going to kill our children. What else could we do?"

Returning to the living room, Sir Dorai said to Rose, "She has suffered enough, poor soul. We need you to evacuate this house, Rose. We will send for your husband and he can help you pack."

He pulled out the map. The dotted "W" held his attention. He knew there had to be an answer. Taking Westby, a soldier, with him, he returned to the base of the well. Westby held the flare while Dorai searched and tapped every stone, his fingers feeling every crack.

"Sir, if you stand back, you can see some of the stones on the wall are darker than others."

Sir Dorai stood back, his eyes traveling over the slabs. Yes, he could see the darker ones.

Westby continued, "Sir, there are some there on the floor, too." On hands and knees, they examined them. The darker stones on the wall and the floor formed a dotted "W," a duplicate of the one on the parchment. Four slabs on the wall and three on the floor made the letter.

"Try putting pressure on all seven stones at once," Sir Dorai directed. They balanced the torch against the ladder. It took some shuffling around and several attempts, but as they coordinated their efforts, the sound of heavy click-

ing developed and the wall by their side slid
back to reveal a gap large enough for a man to
walk through. Westby retrieved the torch
which had fallen as the wall moved. He
directed light into the darkness of the tunnel
and cautiously stepped inside. Sir Dorai
hesitated for a moment then joined him. They
walked a short way and came to a "T" intersec-
tion. "We must go back and get reinforcements," Dorai called to Westby, who had
continued some way along the tunnel to the
left.

"Sir, there is a body here," came the reply.

Sir Dorai hastened in the direction of
Westby's voice. "It is not Leopold. It must be
Samuel. Poor beggar. Westby, we will return to
the widow's house. You will help the family
move out and I will arrange for troops to move
in here. We will not enter the castle without
adequate men."

Sir Dorai calculated Elliad would have at
least 3,000 men with him. He himself would
need as many soldiers as could be spared to
take the castle, that is, if the trickster was still
there. He did not relish a confrontation in the
tunnels, but then to try and scale the walls and
overthrow the castle from without would be a
nigh impossible task.

The afternoon was waning when Sir Dorai
led the soldiers through the opening, along the
shadowy catacombs, and to their immense
surprise, into the throne room.

By the open wall lay piles of Gospel Books. Sir Dorai could not begin to guess the relevance of this. He sent the men to search the castle and see how many people they could find. Within a short space of time the men returned, reporting the towers empty, finding the stables the same.

Trembling groups of aged servants and women with children were brought to the reception room for Sir Dorai to interview. It was now apparent; the rogue had cheated them and flown the nest. The servants declared the flight took place over a week ago.

Shaking uncontrollably, an old man handed over several bunches of keys. They were the keys to the gates and the dungeons. Sir Dorai sent his men down to the cells and they returned with Ruskin and the other five spy-knights. Other prisoners also present in the dungeons were being held for questioning. Food and water left in the dungeons had dwindled to an end the day before.

The servants confirmed there was plenty of food left at the castle as the stocks collected for the siege were still plentiful. Elliad had only been able to carry limited supplies. Sir Dorai sent the servants to the kitchens to make bread and prepare soups and stews for the hungry soldiers. A thorough search of the castle revealed that everything else of value was gone—stolen.

No one knew a thing about Jobyna's whereabouts. Sir Dorai tried to work out a plan of action. He needed information as to which way Elliad journeyed and how many days start the man had on them. In spite of the descending darkness, he sent troops to every border, instructing them to glean information along the way. Messages and orders were dispatched. Half of the troops at Mayhew were ordered to the city, the rest ready to move at any moment. Luke was to stay put at Samdene.

Sir Dorai, deep in thought, was pacing the marble floor of the throne room when Westby appeared by the tunnel opening. "Sir, I believe we've found King Leopold's body. We did not touch it but left it there for you to view."

Sir Dorai followed Westby, not knowing Elliad's feet had also traversed the same ground just some days previous. His heart was heavy as he gazed on the death-stricken face of the king he had loved and served for the sake of the kingdom of Frencolia. The truth was revealed here in this chamber. The king could be laid to rest at last, but he, Dorai, would not rest until his murderer was brought to permanent justice for the crimes he committed against Frencolia.

Examining the cave, Dorai realized Elliad must have been there. A few garments lay on the floor but there was no sign of the treasures King Leopold spoke of in his testament. Sir Dorai ordered the body to be carefully carried to lie in state in the Frencolian throne room, vowing the king's death must be vindicated by Elliad's execution.

19

Sabin ran toward Luke, who was in the throes of mounting a horse. He had decided for exercise he would canter around the courtyard. "Sir Dorai is at the gate, Luke, he will have news!" Luke was instantly fearful. Sir Dorai had come himself. The young man left the horse with Sabin and hurried to the portal where the soldiers were letting down the drawbridge and pulling up the portcullis. Luke imagined the worst. By the time Sir Dorai had crossed the bridge and dismounted, Luke's imagination had been so active he was thinking how he would cope at Jobyna's funeral!

Sir Dorai motioned them inside the Knight's Tower and went at once to the office with Luke and Sir Keith. "Sit down, Your Majesty." Sir Dorai was agitated. "I have both news to your liking and bad news. . . . " He paused as though not sure where to begin.

Luke said quietly, "Give me the good news first and maybe I will be more sustained to take the bad news." Luke was now certain he would hear that Elliad had killed his sister.

"The good news is that Elliad and all his followers have left Frencolia. This in itself is a great victory, a triumph for the kingdom. We have secured possession of the King's Castle. There has been no battle, no soldiers lost." Luke waited. "The bad news, I am sorry to be the one to tell you, Luke," he said, putting aside formality for the sake of the personal nature of the next statement, "is that Elliad, . . . " Luke closed his eyes. " . . . as far as we can tell, has taken your sister, Jobyna, with him as his hostage."

"Then she is still alive?" Luke's face broke into a tremulous smile. He could not see the grave danger ahead for Jobyna. All thoughts of this were overshadowed with relief. *She was still alive!*

Elliad left servants and women in the castle— those too old, unable or unwilling to travel. These people report your sister present at a celebration feast just some hours before they all departed. They say she sat at the table beside Elliad. Dressed like a princess with a diamond

211

tiara on her head, she appeared to be in good health.

"That reminds me. The rest of the disturbing news is that Elliad has taken the treasures of Frencolia with him. Also, we have the body of King Leopold lying in state in the throne room."

Sir Dorai went into the details of his entry to the King's Castle, of the passages being open, even the entry from the tunnel into the throne room and the treasure chamber. Astounded how well Luke took the fact of his sister's kidnapping, Dorai hoped the real reaction was not delayed. He was glad when Luke's positive attitude continued.

The two senior knights listened as Luke said, "God will take care of Jobyna. She will, in God's time, be returned to us."

Sir Dorai told Luke there were many things to consider in Frencolia first, but when those were taken care of, a large army would go and fight, if necessary, for Jobyna's release and bring Elliad to justice. At present, King Leopold's funeral was paramount. His body would lie in state for 10 days and then it would be laid to rest in the tomb of his predecessors. The second important event would be Luke's coronation.

The distance from Samdene in the north to Frencberg in the center of the kingdom, was a matter of three or four hours on horseback. News of Luke's imminent arrival had been announced and thousands of people lined the streets waiting to greet him, hoping to catch a glimpse. News of Elliad's exile, the finding of King Leopold's body, and the boy-king's journey from Samdene were all topics of top priority to talk about and pass on. People waved blossom-covered branches as they saw him coming, and the cry Luke had heard on his journey to Samdene was reiterated, "God bless King Luke Chanec! God bless King Luke Chanec!"

Soldiers, moving on foot on either side of Luke, struggled to keep the crowds from stopping his horse, but the people were happy and there were no unfortunate incidents against Luke or Frencolia. It would have been easier and shorter in distance for Luke to have taken the back roads to the King's Castle, but Sir Dorai led the procession through the main city streets, around the central square and back to the main gate of the castle.

Cheers resounded everywhere and Luke waved to the people, taking time to stop and shake hands when some eager patriots broke through the cordon of soldiers.

"God bless Frencolia, God bless you all," Luke replied to the masses.

Upon his arrival at the castle, Luke was escorted to the throne room where he stood reverently by the bier on which King Leopold lay. He recalled the first time he saw his body. It seemed like a century ago. How he, Luke, had changed since that time. He had grown from a boy to a man. Luke stood, his head bowed, entreating God to grant him wisdom in the mighty task that lay ahead of him.

To Sir Dorai's surprise, Luke knelt and prayed aloud, "Oh, Lord, the task is great. I need Your help." He was silent for several minutes. No one dared move. "Thank You for sparing Jobyna and I pray You will keep her safe. Thank You for bringing us all this far today . . . " Luke continued in prayer for some minutes, ending with, "Amen." Those in that great room joined in the "amen." It was a moving moment.

Sir Dorai directed Luke's attention to the Gospel Books. He had no explanation as to why they were left here in the throne room. Half had been in the tunnel entrance, the others stacked by the dais. Luke was overcome with emotion as his eyes fell on the Gospel Books. "People all over this land have given their lives to protect these. My own father . . . and mother . . . "

A reassuring hand was placed on Luke's shoulder and Dorai spoke with sincerity, "There are some things, Luke, I have not told you. I once was greatly against the Gospel

Book myself. I never would have harmed anyone for their belief in it, but I thought they were all mad, bereft of their senses. I am changing my mind, I don't know what to think any more."

Luke requested he be shown where his sister had been kept while she was at the castle, but it was not certain exactly what section of the castle she had inhabited the last few days before she was taken. Ruskin showed Luke to the room where he had visited Jobyna. It was one of the rooms near the soldiers' quarters, used as a recovery annex for injured soldiers. Luke was relieved when he learned she had not been kept down in the dungeons among the damp and stench. From what the remaining servants could tell, it seemed she had been moved around somewhat and they were never sure which quarters she would be occupying.

Sir Dorai decided to make a full inspection of the castle. He would have men accompany him to make an inventory of the remaining chattels. There was to be a meeting of the lords and senior knights at the castle that evening, but until then, there was nothing pressing to be accomplished. He told Luke he had sent out soldiers to see if they could find which direction

Elliad had gone, but word may not be forthcoming until the next day. Luke decided to tag along on the inspection tour. He could help write down the things that would be needed to refurnish the rooms. Maybe some of the wings could be closed off until needed. That would save the country expense.

They had scarcely begun the inventory when a messenger interrupted them saying, "Your Majesty, Sir Dorai, there are crowds of people at the gates. Shall I let them in?"

"The official time for the people to begin to pay their last respects to King Leopold is not until tomorrow, from sunrise. You know this, man! Why do you ask?" Sir Dorai replied gruffly.

The man bowed humbly. "I am sorry, sir. I have not explained. Sir, the people at the gates have come with gifts for the castle. The news has got around how the false pretender stripped the King's Castle of furnishings and contents and stole the treasures of the kingdom. People are at the gates with all manner of articles. One man has a cart full of furniture."

Luke hastened to greet these people. Their generosity warmed his heart. Some articles were worn with use and time; others were brand new. There were plates, cutlery, vases, pitchers, bowls, rugs, tapestries, furniture, household linen and silks, piled high upon cart after cart. Citizens from Frencberg kept coming and coming. The steady flow continued well after sunset.

Luke thanked each contributor, chatting with them, asking their name, assuring them that if he could ever do something for them, they must ask. Their kindness would be rewarded. He thought of Jobyna, how much she loved to know a person's name, and how well she could remember each one. If only she were here now. He knew she would enjoy meeting these people, hearing their voices, committing their names and faces to memory. As children, it had been a game to memorize people's names and such like. Of course, she had always won.

Sir Dorai had almost completed the inventory, delegating other men to make lists of the goods being brought to the castle. How marvelous the Frencolians were, rallying around Luke at this highly volatile time. He felt the spirit was good and would breed unity among the citizens.

The last rooms to be inspected were the guest apartments at the back of the castle. Sir Dorai had stayed in these chambers some years ago when visiting King Leopold. He checked each room. They too had been stripped of everything of value. The beds were bare and the only other furniture remaining was a small table. Sir Dorai had the other men with him check the rest of the apartments while he walked through the first. He looked through the bedroom and bathroom, calling out what would be needed to make the rooms functional. His scribe wrote quickly. As he passed through the door into the living room, he paused. Noticing the tabletop had a "J" on it, written in what looked like ink, he guessed it must have been drawn by Jobyna's hand.

Dorai thoughtfully examined the table top. At some stage Jobyna must have occupied this apartment. What significance did the "J" have? He was going to send someone off to fetch Luke, then he thought better of it. It would not be good to raise the boy's hopes. He ordered the men to search every inch of the room. Jobyna may have wished Luke to know she had been here. But then, she had ink. Maybe she wrote a message under the table on the wood. Sir Dorai turned the table upside down. Nothing! A full 10 minutes passed before a soldier discovered the upside down "J" on the door. They had looked everywhere—in the fireplace, the empty wall-cupboards, everywhere there was to look.

The bedroom door was pushed open and an observant soldier exclaimed, "Hey, there's a letter on the door, like on the table, but upside down!" They all rushed to the door. The soldier was standing bent at the waist, scratching his head which was twisted to observe the "J" the right way up. While in this almost upside down position, his face going red, he declared, "There's a ledge up there, I can see it, if you bend over and put your head like this, you'll see it and . . . "

"Okay, we can see it quite well as we are, man," interrupted Sir Dorai. "Get the table over here. Quickly, I say!"

A soldier moved the table under the transom. Climbing up on it, he reached up and felt along the ledge. His fingers grasped the parchment and the letter was retrieved. Sir Dorai, fingers shaking, opened the scroll and read it. With great satisfaction, he took it to Luke.
"Dearest Brother Luke," he read,

> By the time you receive this, I will be far away. I pray you will read this with thanks in your heart and not bitterness. Remember Joseph in the Gospel Book. Think if he had never been stolen away to Egypt. God is in control. Our lives are not a series of mistakes, but appointments God makes for us. E. is treating me well now. In the past few weeks, my life has been spared many times. By just cutting a thin thread, God could have taken me to be with Father and Mother in heaven. I believe I shall stand on Frencolian soil again, brother. Do not grieve, only trust. My prayers are with you constantly.

Then came the closing words with the under-lining here and there.

The letter brought relief to Luke's heavy heart. He remembered the jeweled case and the scroll he had left with Jobyna in the valley. She must have hidden the case in a rocky cleft and this cryptic message held the clues necessary for him to find it. Sir Dorai sent 20 trusted men to search the valley cliffs, and as expected, they returned with the jeweled case containing the Gospel Book, maps and charts.

The pieces of the puzzle were slowly slipping into place. Luke realized Jobyna must have read and studied the papers before leaving the valley. He shuddered to think how Elliad had obtained the information from her. The words "E. is treating me well now" betrayed some of what she must have suffered.

Luke echoed Sir Dorai's vow. Elliad must be brought swiftly to the end he deserved. "The Gospel Book says in several places, 'He who leads into captivity shall go into captivity; he who kills with the sword must be killed with the sword.'

"We will take care of Frencolia first and then we will see my sister returned home and the evil Elliad brought to justice," Luke vowed. It pleased Sir Dorai to hear these words. He believed that his support of Luke as king of Frencolia was for the good of the kingdom.

After the evening meal, Sir Dorai addressed the group, turning to Luke first. "Your Majesty, King Luke Chanec of Frencolia, lords, fellow knights, I have somewhat of a confession to make tonight. Most of you are aware of what I am to tell you, so I will address my words to Luke.

"Many years ago, King Leopold wanted to marry my only sister who was a few years younger than myself. She was betrothed to another, a close friend, a cousin to Leopold. She would not break this betrothal, and the king married another, Estelle. I was furious, both with my sister and her fiancee. I was young and proud. It would have suited me to have my sister be queen in Frencolia. I told them I would never speak to them again. The years passed. They had several children and were very prosperous. Then the Evangelist came. I would not listen to him and was more obstinate about it when my sister and her husband accepted the teachings. My brother-in-law became much loved by the people and he became very wealthy. I was jealous. He gave up his role as a senior knight and was no longer close to King Leopold. I decided to disown them, that is, my sister and her husband. I told no one I was related to them. I regret these past decisions greatly, Luke, for you see, my sister, Elissa, was your mother." He paused, waiting for these words to sink into Luke's mind.

Luke's parents had never spoken of Sir Dorai. He had no idea they were related, and he was overcome with surprise. Jobyna and he had a living relative! An uncle. Luke was not angry at all with Sir Dorai, but rather, was delighted to know the truth.

"I was deeply overcome with sorrow and anger when Elissa and Chanec were murdered. It has tormented me greatly to think if maybe I had supported them more, this may not have come to pass. I can only ask you to forgive me for supporting such a traitor as Elliad and believe me when I say I desire to see him pay for what he has done. I will leave no stone unturned to see your sister, Jobyna, my niece, safely returned to Frencolia."

The following morning at dawn, the front gates to the King's Castle were propped open and all successive doors to the throne room likewise. They would remain so for 10 days, open both day and night. All in the kingdom were welcome to come and pay their last respects to King Leopold. Soldiers forming a guard of honor would stand shoulder to shoulder from the moat bridge to the bier, standing four hours at a time in six shifts around the clock. A black velvet cloth covered the throne and dais. Luke, as heir, was expected to be on hand to greet kingdom officials, barons, dukes and knights. Sir Dorai would be presented as the king's uncle and guardian.

Luke had never been given any training or grooming for the job of being a king. Sir Dorai told him just to be himself. This was the best advice Luke could ever ask for and he paid heed to it. The people loved him. He was so much "on the level"—one they could identify with—one who had shared the heartaches of the past two years with them. Those who met him personally spread the word of his natural empathy with their suffering kinsfolk. King Leopold had heavily taxed the kingdom and was known for his love of money. He was considered a tyrant, not as Elliad was for violence and evil, but for his heavy taxing, which made the poor poorer and the rich richer. Many of the people who came to pay their last respects to Leopold, were in reality trying to catch a glimpse of Luke. They brought gifts with them, offered kind words of encouragement, condolence and sympathy for the death of his parents, and expressed distaste regarding the dreadful news of Jobyna's kidnapping.

Luke's reception room was becoming cluttered with potted plants, young trees for planting in the castle gardens, golden plates and silver chalices, beautiful tapestries and rugs, all gifts to Luke. Some of the wealthier barons and dukes brought bags and chests of coin and gold pieces. Sir Valdre dealt with these matters, writing down the gift and the giver's name.

Luke was introduced to baron's wives and children. He tried hard to memorize names but found himself forever apologizing when he forgot. Constantly reminded of Jobyna and her love of people, the new king wished she could be here. She would be in her element.

At the same time Luke was dealing with all of these visitors, knights were returning from Border Castles and Knight's Towers. There had been no sightings of Elliad and his company of knights, soldiers and servants. Luke began to realize he would not know the route Elliad had taken. He was trying to come to terms with this fact when a knight came with a report from a shepherd located in the hills near Ahren, not far from the eastern border of Frencolia.

The shepherd had informed the knights of a large company of mounted soldiers, people on carts and wagons, all moving eastward. He had seen them cross the border at dawn and had wondered if it was a strange dream. This was the answer Sir Dorai had been waiting for. Now they knew the direction Elliad had taken. He had pursued the shortest, most obscure route out of the country. Sir Dorai was sure Elliad's journey would be slow. Speed would be impeded by the number of servants, women and children he had taken with him. People in villages along the way would be able to tell Frencolian scouts that they had passed by. A company that large could not go unnoticed. The council felt sure Elliad would head for a country hostile to Frencolia, using the stolen treasures to buy himself liberty to live there. Sir Dorai reassured himself that there were kingdom affairs to attend to in Frencolia first. Then it was just a matter of time before they caught up with Elliad and made him pay.

Partway through the fourth day of vigil, Luke was approached by one of the knights appointed to organize those who wished an audience with him. "Your Majesty, there is a man from Mayhew. He is a doctor and says he would like to talk to you about your sister. He will not speak with anyone else but you, Sire."

Luke asked to have him shown to the chamber he was using as a reception room. Like shadows, his two bodyguards, Loran and Granville, followed him closely. Luke had thought he would never get used to having these men with him constantly, but to his amazement, he did not notice them now. They were there if he needed them, and when he didn't, he seemed to look past them and get on with his duties. Sabin was a wonderful helper, running back and forth with messages, looking after Luke's well-being and keeping the boy to the unwritten schedule.

225

Sabin announced the doctor, "Doctor Gilbert, of Mayhew."

Apprehensively, Gilbert entered the room. He was wary of Loran and Granville, standing either side of the chair Luke occupied. Gilbert bowed low.

Luke and Gilbert conversed for over an hour. The brother was horrified to learn of Elliad's trickery, using the fictitious "John" to bribe and torment his beloved sister. He realized the intimidation that Gilbert had been subjected to and assured the doctor of his forgiveness and pardon. Thanking him for coming forward with this information, Luke also showed gratitude for the way the doctor had cared for Jobyna.

"Your sister is the bravest person I have ever met." Gilbert said seriously, tears clouding his brown eyes. Gilbert told Luke if he, the king, was in need of medical attention at any time, he would be prepared to offer his services.

Luke had Sabin fetch one of the Gospel Books. He gave it to Gilbert. "This is where Jobyna finds her strength, Gilbert. Promise me you will read this book." Gilbert took the book from Luke. "I have forgiven you, Gilbert, and I know Jobyna will have, too. What has been said between us will stay within these walls. But before you have full release from your guilt, you need God's forgiveness."

Before they parted, Gilbert turned to the boy. With a grave voice, he asked Luke how he, personally and emotionally, was coping with his sister's abduction. Looking into the doctor's sad eyes, Luke replied with assurance, "God is giving me strength and faith. It is great sustenance to know Jobyna trusts God. As for me, I will serve the Lord and trust Him."

20

As the day of Luke's coronation drew closer, the soon-to-be-crowned king dispatched Gospel Books and messages to every town and village. He called for a time of prayer and fasting and had God's Words from the Second Book of Chronicles 7:14 written on each letter: "If my people, which are called by my name, shall humble themselves, and pray, and seek my face, and turn from their wicked ways; then will I hear from heaven, and will forgive their sin, and will heal their land."

The Gospel Books were to be read in the village and town squares. Those who had books in their homes were to read them aloud to their families and households. Each message was closed with the words, "I, Luke Chanec, King of Frencolia, believe the word of the Gospel Book to be the only hope for this country."

The messages were received with great understanding and rejoicing by the Christians in Frencolia. All other citizens, the majority, were happy to accept that the reign of terror was over. Elliad had been cruel to everyone in his way, and destroyed or used people as if they were disposable. Compliance with Luke Chanec's requests posed no problem. King Leopold had squeezed, often in underhanded and dishonest ways, to get money even from the poorest of the poor. The people were ready to accept a new king, though young, who would rule with kindness and honesty. Even though he was religious, it would be a nice change from tyranny. Those who would have violently opposed Luke and his Christian beliefs had left the country with Elliad.

Manor houses had been left empty by knights loyal to the exile. Luke planned to allocate these to needy families. There was so much to be done to restore the kingdom to sensible law and order.

Luke's coronation was a great time of celebration and festivity, a triumph in Frencolia. The boy rehearsed the coronation ceremony. Every movement and word was repeated until Luke was comfortable and relaxed. The crown and scepter were retrieved from the secret cavity under the dais step. Sir Dorai was thankful Elliad had not got his hands on those items.

The day was clear and beautiful, an early taste of summer. Special robes had been prepared for Luke to wear, but these served only to make him apprehensive. For the first time since his acceptance at the Knight's Tower near Mayhew, Luke had doubts. He was barely 16. Was he really doing the right thing? What right did he, Luke, son of Chanec of Chanoine, have to the throne of Frencolia? Did God want him to be king in Frencolia? Luke needed someone to talk to.

The boy had fasted for the last three days, and Sabin had now encouraged him to eat something to sustain him before the pressure of this great day fell. The servant entered the suite where Luke was deep in contemplation, worrying about the day ahead.

"Sabin, I have grave fears. I do not know if I can go through with the coronation with all the reservations I have." Sabin stared at him. Luke continued, "I have no one I can talk with. If only Father . . . " He gestured helplessly, closing his eyes, trying to control his emotions.

Sabin spoke with reassurance. "Luke, my master's son, remember the words your father quoted so often: 'God removes kings and sets

230

up kings.' Also, 'By me kings reign, and princes decree justice.' If your father were alive today, he would have to agree that God's hand is in your coming to the throne of Frencolia to be crowned king. This is none of man's doing. This is not your doing, Luke. Even apart from the seal, you are nearest heir to the throne. The plan is God's. Your fears are not from God. You must have triumph over your fears. Did not Jobyna write that if we trust God, then there are no mistakes, only appointments with God? If this is true, then your coronation today is an appointment set by God!"

Luke sat with his head bowed. These were the words he needed to hear. He must pray for strength from the Lord God, and not depend upon himself. Sabin waited while Luke prayed silently.

To the servant's great surprise, Luke rose, put his arms around him, and hugged him close. "Hold me, Sabin, like Father would have. I need counsel. Thank you for your help. Please be there when I need you. The task to help this country weighs heavily upon me and I cannot do it alone." Sabin put his arms about Luke's shoulders, promising his unfailing support. It was a moment that would stay with them for the rest of their lives.

Luke was crowned King Luke Chanec of the kingdom of Frencolia that day. The pomp and ceremony was secondary to the thoughts in Luke's mind. Thoughts of his father who indeed, had quoted again and again the words in the Gospel Book, that God was the One who set up kings. As Luke walked from the royal suite, along the corridors, through the reception room and into the throne room, all lined with knights, barons, dukes and officials, he allowed Jobyna's words to run through his mind. "This, today, is not a mistake, it is an appointment. God is in control!"

He walked up the steps of the dais and turned to sit on the throne. As he had rehearsed, he stood for a moment, then sat.

The scepter and the crown were handed by Sir Dorai to the five lords and each held them for a while, publicly giving Luke their blessing and pledge of support. Lord Farey, after kissing the scepter, handed it to Luke, then placed the crown on the king's head. Officially, Luke Chanec was now king of Frencolia.

All the officials knelt before him and Sir declared, "God bless King Luke Chanec, of Frencolia. Long may he reign."

one else in the throne room proclaimed, ss King Luke Chanec." The cry was down the hall, in the reception room, stle courtyard, and the great cheerple outside the castle gates could en the noise had died down somewhat, Luke stood by the great throne for a moment, then he knelt. Words he had memorized from the book of First Chronicles 29:11–13 were fervently quoted by the new king of Frencolia:

Thine, O Lord, is the greatness, and the power, and the glory, and the victory, and the majesty: for all that is in the heaven and in the earth is thine; Thine is the kingdom, O Lord, and thou art exalted as head above all. Both riches and honour come of thee, and thou reignest over all; and in thine hand is power and might; and in thine hand it is to make great, and to give strength unto all. Now therefore, our God, we thank thee, and praise thy glorious name.

Luke rose, motioning for all in the throne room to rise. The king walked down the steps, out of the throne room, through the reception room, out of the castle and into the courtyard. He mounted the horse held ready for him. Sabin and Sir Dorai were at either side. The five lords followed and then the knights. The procession rode through the streets of Frencberg, around the square, and back to the King's Castle. Excitement among the crowds was deafening. Luke had a hard job keeping his horse calm. The crown almost fell off his head once as his horse shied.

Finally the processional was over. Thankful to be back in the relative calm of the castle walls, Luke beheld the celebration dinner set out in the great courtyard. The lords sat at the table with Luke, under a great canopy, the senior knights at another table close by. Everyone else stood to eat. Never before had there been such a feast. It was a day never to be forgotten.

There was triumph in Frencolia.

What are Elliad's evil plans?

What will become of Jobyna?

Who is "The Crazy Prince?"

These questions and others
will be answered in
Castles,
Book 2 of *The Frencolian Chronicles*.
Available in the summer of 1991.

For additional copies of
Treasures
or information on other titles in
The Frencolian Chronicles,
contact your local Christian bookstore or
call Christian Publications, toll-free,
1-800-233-4443.